Scenery of Dreams

Morag Henriksen

Scenery of Dreams

Morag Henriksen

Author:	Henriksen, Morag
Subjects:	Short stories.
	Scotland -- Fiction.
ISBN	9780980838534
Dewey Number	823.92

Printed by Clays Ltd, a St Ives Group Company, London

ACKNOWLEDGEMENTS

To all the friends, who helped and encouraged me to publish some of the stories I have told them, many thanks, especially to Brian Donaghy , Scott and Steph Henriksen, and Cailean Maclean.

The title of the book is a quotation from a letter by Robert Louis Stevenson and the idea in *Over the Sea* that place-names in Lochalsh and Wester Ross equate to those of the classical Underworld, came from W. Comyns Beaumont, eccentric journalist and British Israelite, via my English teacher, W.A.Ross (Willie WAR), who used to tease West Coast pupils with it.

Stories and poems published previously:

Landscape with Figures	*Scotsman Magazine Tale-ender 1*
Saved	*Nomad 13*
Christmas Dinner	*McGregor's Gathering Short Story Competition*
The Tairsgeir	*McGregor' s Gathering Short Stories BBC Books*
Johnny Com	*Skyeviews 6*
Facts of Life	*RAW 11*
Orange and Blues	*West Coast Magazine 1*
Western Island	*Island 4*
Mrs Millar	*Carranach 55*
Stille Nacht	*Skyeviews 3, Northwords 4*
Aignish	*Siud an t-Eilean ed. Ian Stephen, Acair*
A Jersey For My Son	*Skyeviews 3*

Art work . . . Morag Henriksen
Art Editor . . Scott Henriksen
Editor . . . Brian Donaghy

Contents

AOIBHNEAS

Out on the moor one day
When I was young
I had a sudden vision of infinity.
I stood upon the shimmering hill,
my sandals scuffed with heather dust
and saw the morning.
The larks were up
pouring their music down the sparkling air.
The ocean held its breath
And suddenly
there in my kilt,
my scratched brown knees,
my pigtails,
I felt that I could fly.
Joy caught
and tossed my spirits
high,
sky-high.
Delight erupted.
My awareness leaped
the obstacles of earthly vision.
Laughing, I ran
in touch for one brief moment
with the light,
the blaze and essence
of the universe.

LANDSCAPE WITH FIGURES

THE mountain stood above the village; the village straggled along the road and beyond the road lay the sea. A three-tiered landscape so sharply delineated that the children in the school painted only one kind of picture. There was no other picture to paint.

"Now, children, today I want you to draw anything you like. Use your imaginations."

Today I will make the perfect picture. At the top of the page I must put a row of wavy brown hills – or maybe a big brown lump like Morbheinn at the back of the school. Sun in the top left-hand corner to fill the space.

Below the brown hill I will put a fence to separate the moor from the green fields. Put strokes for the rushes on the crofts. Now I'm ready for the houses. Make them all the same, side by side. I'll need a pencil for this – a door in the centre, windows to right and left, quartered neatly and curtained at the sides,

two more above with triangles in the roof for storm windows. Chimneys at each
gable with a curly plume of smoke on the left where the kitchen is.

I think I'll do slates on the roof. That'll take a while. Ballachulish slates –
blue-grey and shiny in the wet. Now I'll put roses round the door and on either
side of the path and I'm ready for the road. A long black strip for the tar and a
green strip beside it for the grass.

Perhaps I'll put in the telegraph poles – no, I won't bother.

Good. Now dot, dot, dot with the crayon to make the shingle on the shore and
there's space at the bottom for the blue sea and maybe Captain's boat.

I've finished. There's a picture. That's the real world. What is there to
imagine?"

MISS MacKay cycled sedately along the road on her way to school.
She had been doing the same journey, two hundred days in the year, for
twenty years. Her hair had gone grey under her sensible hat and her
joints had grown stiff as she turned the pedals.

She was very stout. Her bicycle was of the heavy upright kind with a
basket on the handlebars and a fan of neat cords protected her skirt from
the spokes of the rear wheel.

She braked as always just before the school gate and, not quite
stopping, hopped off and ran a little with her machine.

The infants watched her in awe through the railings. One day, maybe,
she would forget to jump off in time and the bicycle would carry her east
along the road and away and away out of sight forever.

She scolded them into their lines as the whistle blew. Inside the classroom her kindly round face became fierce; her voice, quite soft at home,
became shrill and domineering. Miss MacKay had put on her overall.
She was about to teach.

"Two ones two. Two twos four. Two threes six. Two fours eight."
The infants sang about her, chanting hypnotically.

There was a sort of sexual pleasure in standing dreamily round Miss
MacKay's high desk, watching her toying with a piece of chalk, turning
it over and over, pressing the point into the grooves in the wood, mind
drifting away . . .

What a big front she has – like a shelf. I bet you could balance a sixpence on it. No. A shilling.

"MARY MACKENZIE!"

A screech shattered the atmosphere. Cold trickles of fear ran down your legs.

"Stop your daydreaming this minute and tell me what are two sevens."

Miss Mackay's voice would shatter a bottle. Her soporific chanting punctuated by violent yells was calculated to destroy the nerves of the most placid infant.

"Please Miss, I thought you was a lion," A wee boy complained, terrified one day by a sudden roar.

The ritual tables over – ritual reading. To make sure they *knew* their books Miss MacKay revised not once but three or four times.

Come come come

Come to Mother, Pat

Come to Mother, Ann.

Pat ran to Mother.

Ann ran to Pat.

Pat comes to Mother.

Ann comes to Pat.

The infants have it off pat.

Miss MacKay, who is patter than Pat, gazes out of the high window across the blue sea to the hills on the southern shore. The sunlight twinkles on the water. Captain is rowing out for his net.

It would be nice to be out there free of routine, free of the timetable, free of the clock. The young slim girl stirs inside Miss MacKay, forgetting the elderly, imprisoning fat. She runs down to the shore, her hair streaming in the wind; she stands on tiptoe by the lapping waves and the big-booted seaman clasps her to his rough jersey. He picks her up and carries her out to . . . .

"Donnie MacRae, stop picking your nose this minute! And eating it too! You filthy boy, go and stand in the corner."

Miss MacKay, spinster of this parish, cycles home after school to her neat villa called Morbheinn. Her home is the model for every infant's drawing. Maybe it was copied from one.

In the small sunless kitchen built against the rock sits her aged father. Once he was a Highland bobby in Glasgow, a hard man; now he sits by the fire rubbing olive oil into his arthritic hands, rubbing, rubbing all day long.

He still thinks of her as his bonnie wee lassie, his treasure, but he has guarded her too close. No man will carry her off now.

She consoles herself with the cosy romances in *The People's Friend* and knitting patterns for lacy jumpers.

On Sundays she teaches in Sabbath School. The children trudge along the street to meet her in church, stiff with pigtails, hats and gloves. They talk in solemn whispers as befits the Lord's Day, or practise their repetition under their breath, squinting quickly at the words then casting eyes upwards, boots pounding to the rhythm.

> *I to the hills will lift mine eyes*
> *From whence doth come mine aid...*

Miss MacKay hides it well but she has a strong sense of humour. When she laughs silently her eyes close up like slits behind her owly glasses and her bosoms jiggle up and down. Imaginary sixpences fall in showers.

Two little girls are walking to church with her, clutching sweaty Bibles and pennies for the heathens in Africa.

"I've got a budgie."

"Have you, dear? That's nice."

"Yes and its name is Joey."

"Does it lay eggs?"

"No. It's not married."

"You ass, Katie!" says her little sister. "Mammie's married and she doesn't lay eggs!"

Miss MacKay's bosoms shoogle with delight. She treasures the story to tell over the teacups in the staff room.

MISS MacKay's father died one day – the arthritic hands seized up forever – and the children examined her carefully to see what it felt like to have a dead father. But she looked just the same.

Then the infants were assembled with the big ones to give Miss MacKay a clock, which she said she had always wanted. And after that they never saw Miss MacKay again.

Maybe she went to Inverness like they said or perhaps, just perhaps, her bicycle carried her along the road east, away and away to the lands beyond the morning where the real lions roar.

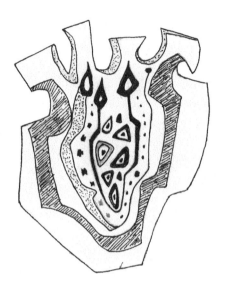

THE BURNING FIERY FURNACE

A T the side of the school between the bicycle shed and the staffroom window lay the coke heap. You had to pass it on your run round to the girls' lavvies. The coke fed the furnace which lurked in a grim hole, blacker than darkness, beside the headmaster's room. Big boys stoked it and my father, the headmaster and Bella Charlie, the school cleaner, dealt with its sulks and its subtleties.

I did not like the furnace room. It smelt poisonously of sulphur and dust and its darkness was so intense that even electric light, when it came, did nothing to dispel the thick shadows in its corners. It seemed to have no angles like a proper room – just a circle of dusk round the monster of iron that squatted to one side of the door, its bandy legs permanently surrounded by its crunchy fodder, its stovepipe disappearing from the middle of its back up into the high gloom of the roof.

I seldom went near it but I stared at it often in my mind – the burning fiery furnace – and wondered how they managed to fit Shadrach,

Mesach and Abednego in at the wee door. They must have had to lie down to squeeze in and then, once in, how did they walk about in the midst of the flames with their hats and coats and all on? They must have been able to shrink like Alice in Wonderland. Of course, where the Son of God was involved anything was possible.

But how did they do it?

I used to imagine Nebuchadnezzar standing at the top of the coke-hole steps in all his gorgeous Babylonian robes, his beard and his funny hat ordering Tommy Burran to keep on shovelling coke till the shimmering heat from the dragon's belly blistered him to a frazzle while the cheerful mini-men walked about unscathed in its white-hot core.

I HAD a strictly fundamentalist upbringing. The Bible was the literal truth. I had psalms to learn and stories to remember every day but Saturday. I also had a vividly pictorial imagination so that when my father intoned, *Set a watch upon our tongues and on our thoughts* at family worship I would imagine the big silver watch in his waistcoat on the back of my tongue. I tried sticking my finger down my throat to get the feel of it, gave myself the dry bokes and got a dunt from my mother for misbehaving at the prayer. I knew better than to ask why ever we would want God to do such a thing.

My literal mind led me into another spot of bother. For a while I had been puzzling over another of my father's prayerful catchphrases. *"Cast your bread upon the waters and it will return not unto you empty."*

I thought about this all the way home one day as we pushed my sister in her pram down the long street from the shop. A half-loaf of fresh bread was lying wrapped in tissue paper at her feet. It looked like a whole loaf to me but everyone called it a half-loaf.

What would happen, I wondered, if I cast it on the waters? Perhaps it would return as a whole loaf. Then everyone would be pleased and we might have toast at the fireside.

I watched my chance and while my mother was seeing to the baby, I sneaked the loaf out of the house, across the road and down the shore.

With high hopes I threw it in the sea. And watched it settle and sink.

My heart sank with it. I left the seagulls to their feast and trailed back up to the house. I was in for it now.

But strangely, my parents said very little when I confessed at the tea-table. I could almost have thought they were trying not to laugh.

THE OUTSIDE LAVVIES

THE school was an ugly building standing in a beaten earth playground against the green slopes of the raised beach about a quarter of a mile to the east of the village.

The spent ripples of Bauhaus thinking had washed up on its shores to give the new school some enlightenment in the form of big metal-framed windows in place of the poky Victorian Gothic of the earlier school, but repressive Victorian ways of thinking die hard in the Highlands and the windows with their broad windowsills were set so high that even adults had to crane their necks to see out.

Nor had the enlightened architect seen fit to put inside lavatories into the school except for the staff, who had the marvellous luxury of a plastic toilet seat and a cute little wash-hand-basin in the corner.

I sneaked the use of it whenever I could – not as any kind of challenge to authority but just because I liked it. That I could go in there at all was because I was the headmaster's daughter. My sister and I often waited for my father and mother after school to walk home the short distance together. But I would never have dreamed of imposing on this status during school hours. I ran round the gable end to the outside lavvies like everybody else, gaining freedom, exercise and fresh air in the process.

The outside lavvies were fascinating – repellent and yet attractive to us all. They were old – much older than the school. The walls were built of the same drystane as part of the playground wall but at some time a wish for more privacy between boys and girls had caused the old wall to be pointed and built up with a cheap-looking cement screen about a brick thick. This left a fine rampart on the inside of the girls' wall – just the thing for defending against invaders and I did not rest until I had realised my ambition and irritated the boys of my class beyond all endurance so that they stormed our barricades one morning interval.

Normally they would not have dared. An unspoken taboo and fear of the belt kept us off each other's territories but that day the blood was up. Willie Dolan came hurtling over the wall just the way I'd visualised it, a barefoot berserker waving the coke-shovel while the girls shrieked and skirled and clung to each other and I danced and yelled at my pigtailed troops to defend themselves, to fight back, to repel the savage invaders.

I had never been to the cinema in those days but my brain was over-heated with reading fiction. Anything I could lay my hands on I read whether I understood it or not. I used to creep back into school to get at the old Coats' Library. J.P. Coats of Paisley, the cotton king, had tried to be another Carnegie to the schools of Scotland and had supplied each with a glass-fronted cupboard full of inspiring fiction for young minds.

Nobody wanted to read these wordy old empire-builders except me, who was always ravenous for the printed word: *Ungava*, *Deer-slayer*, *Coral Island*, *Masterman Ready*, *Last of the Mohicans* – I read them all, ready or not. I suffered from acute indigestion of the mind and probably did myself more harm than good. Scunnered of Scott and sickened of Dickens, I am everlastingly grateful that I never came across Jane Austen until I was in university, when she had the freshness of sorbet after a heavy meal and gave me back my appetite.

Authority took a dim view of our cavortings in the toilets. They could not see that the coke-shovel was a cutlass and the toilet wall a rampart. Punishments ensued but it was worth it.

There was some obscure adult thing lurking behind the disapproval of our game on the lavatory walls. It was not explained. Sex was the great taboo – so obscure that I remained more or less oblivious to it for most of my childhood.

The big girls in the junior secondary often giggled and locked them-selves in the lavvies but that was their silliness and who would want to do that when the clean air was all about us in the wide playground and we could run and leap with the wind?

Curiosity one Saturday made me put a toe in the crevice of the wall and hoist myself up to look over into the boys' side. I was astonished that it was so beautiful. Instead of our ugly row of smelly closets they had an open space, a sort of sink into which tinkling water poured, over-flowed and cascaded down the rocky slope to a drain near the school wall. It was all so fresh. They had only two green-painted doors with latches while we had four but most wonderful of all, their whole wall and the area around their 'fountain' was covered with ferns and mosses and purple ivy-leaved toadflax.

I was filled with envy. Once again the boys seemed to have all the luck.

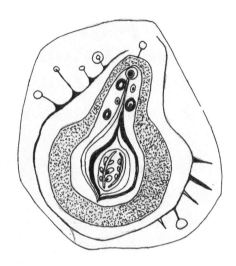

FACTS OF LIFE

"DO you know where babies come from?" Maggie leaned forward. Her breath smelled rank and Joey drew back a little.

"I don't know. I never really thought about it."

The moss was soft by the side of the burn and overhead the wires swooped and sang.

"Haven't you wondered?"

"Mam got Jimmy in the hospital. I went to see her with Dad. It was snowing and I got an apple. I was sick in the train."

"No. I mean how babies get born. Don't you know?"

"I don't like babies. They're boring. I'm not like you – always pushing prams and things."

"I want to be a nurse when I grow up." Maggie was prim.

"Well, I want to be a merchant seaman but I don't expect they'll have me."

"You don't know about babies, do you?"

"I don't think so"

"I'll tell you then." Maggie snuggled closer and her voice took on a moist confidential whisper. "Well – a woman has a round thing and a man has a long thing and the man puts his thing in like this. . . ."

She made a ring with her left forefinger and thumb and poked her other forefinger through, chanting as she did so:

> *"In days of old when men were bold*
> *and women were not invented*
> *men dug holes in telegraph poles*
> *and had to be contented."*

Joey looked at her in amazement. Was she kidding?

"Now, I'll be Nurse Maggie. You lie down flat and open your legs. Close your eyes."

The rough March grass smelled sweet and urgent. Wild daffodils grew in random clumps.

Maggie picked one and laid it on the patient's belly. Sticky juice dripped on her skirt.

"Now you say, 'Doctor, will it be long now?'"

Joey obeyed, giggling.

"You mustn't giggle. Do it right."

"Doctor, will it be long now?"

"No, Mrs MacKay. It'll soon be over. Now say, Ooh! Ooh! Nurse, what is it?"

"Ooh! Ooh! Nurse, what is it?"

Maggie drew the daffodil down Joey's pleated tartan skirt and out between her brown battle-scarred knees.

"It's a boy!"

Joey looked.

"No it's not. It's a daffodil. I've just had a daffodil!"

"Joey Mackenzie! You're not playing it properly. Stop laughing!"

"Well. It's a daft game. Long things and round things! You don't expect me to believe stuff like that."

The giggles turned to a full-throated uproar. She rolled around on the grassy bank, flattening the daffodils, hooting and shrieking. Long legs waved in the air. Her kilt flew about exposing sturdy navy knickers.

Tears ran down her cheeks and she sobbed, "Men dug ho-ho-holes. Honestly! Who told you that? You didn't believe them, surely?"

Maggie's face was crimson too.

"Joey Mackenzie! I'm never going to play with you ever again! Never! And I'm never telling you anything any more. Ever, ever again!" She ran.

Joey lay on her back and gazed into the blue air. Moor fires were scenting the breeze and life was rich. Telegraph poles marched along the roadside and dwindled into the distance. Their secrets hummed a tune on the wires.

> "In days of old when men were bold
> and women were not invented. . . "

Telegraph poles in the Garden of Eden?
What rubbish!

ENTERTAINING STRANGERS

TWO men from the east came along the road one day and stopped at our door. Many people did this – tramps, tinkers, tradesmen, friends. These men fitted none of these categories. They were just strangers.

My mother had gone off on her bicycle to collect the pail of milk from outside Dolan's shop and Dad and I were pottering in the shed when the strangers came.

Tall, thin men, tanned and rangy, they had an outdoor look and it did not seem at all surprising that they asked us for a little meths to light their primus stove.

They were camping up beyond Tulloch, they said, and had no hope of getting any methylated spirits because it was half-day at the shops.

My father felt sorry for them and was quite keen to help them out of their predicament and I, always eager to help my Dad, trotted into the house, fetched a tall stool and climbed up to the highest shelf in the scullery where the meths was kept to be out of my reach. I loved its translucent purple and I stood enjoying it for a while, holding the bottle against the light before hurrying back to where my Dad was talking to the men.

They were very grateful and insisted on paying something, respectable fellows that they were. Coins chinked despite my father's protests and then they went away. We returned to our tasks, smug with our good deed. We did not watch where the men went when they reached the road.

Teatime came and my mother did not return. Still being important and helpful, I went in to lay the table. My father was getting edgy. It was not like my mother to go gallivanting and miss teatime. I stared at the empty plates hungrily. A faint blur of worry began to dull the edge of our hunger pangs. My father began to get food out in a fidgety way. I did not like this at all. Things were not normal.

It was nearly seven o' clock before she skidded to a halt at the gate.

"You have no idea what it's like up the village," she said. "There's these two men, mad drunk, crazy with drink. They're terrorizing the place. The folk in the New Houses had to lock their doors against them. I came round the corner at the hotel slap into them. They made a grab at me and I pedalled for all I was worth straight into the garage. If it hadn't been for Jockie and Farquhar coming to my rescue I don't know what would have happened . . .

"They've been rampaging all over the place. They're mad because the barman locked them out of the pub. I didn't dare come out of the garage until they went off up the street. Goodness knows what they are doing now!

"The thing is – nobody knows where they got so much drink at this time of day. I don't know when I've been so scared and I've spilt all the milk."

She burst into tears.

We did not hear the sequel until the next day because we lived so far out of the village. The men had gone their riotous way up the long street, bawling and cursing and challenging the world to a fight. Everywhere doors shut, locks clicked, curtains twitched. The street lay bare before them.

They went a whole mile before they came to an open door.

The Strict Presbyterians were holding a prayer meeting and were well into the first psalm when the two heroes arrived. The beadle was just stowing the collection into his canvas bag when they barged past him. They roared up the aisle demanding a fight. The singing quavered into silence, the people froze to their seats in horror and the elder in the lectern box wished he wasn't so conspicuous.

Clutching his takings, the beadle made for the police station, wobbling along on his postie's bike. Back he came with Jock the Bobby and, with the law on its side, the congregation rose up in wrath and overpowered the men.

For the first time in many years the cells had inmates. Jock was so unaccustomed to entertaining guests at His Majesty's pleasure that he felt it was all wrong not to give them proper hospitality. He could not help but be kind. They had a terrible blinder on and he knew they would be parched with thirst in the morning, so, when he found a bottle of milk in their pockets he did not take it from them.

"Poor things. They'll need it when they waken up with the dickens of a hangover," he thought.

Instead of subsiding into a drunken stupor, his prisoners grew more and more uproarious. They sang and yelled and cursed all night. Jock couldn't understand it.

In the morning when they had finally collapsed with exhaustion Jock investigated their milk bottle. He should have smelt it sooner. It reeked of methylated spirits. The story went round the village like wildfire.

When my father and I heard it we looked at each other for the flash of a second, then we too shook our heads.

Yes. Who could have given them the meth?

Who could have been so stupid?

STILLE NACHT

I FIRST became aware of Christmas, in Alness, in a house called Omdurman, named after a battlefield and crammed with cousins. There was a tree and tinsel and presents and parties, all things strange to me, a child of wartime austerity and Strict Presbyterian upbringing. Over on the east coast, among my mother's family, my parents seemed different somehow, lighter and brighter.

Everyone talked about Christmas and nobody explained it at all. In the hubbub of the crowded house I was left to watch and wonder.

It was all very strange but strangest of all was that on Christmas Eve two German prisoners of war came to share our supper.

Hort and Gert were kindly men, missing their families, slightly ill at ease. I have a vivid memory of them dressed in clumsy grey uniforms, sitting on hardwood chairs in the middle of the family circle around the stove.

We children kept to the back of the grown-ups, peering round chairs and under elbows, shy and suspicious. These were Germans, the enemy, friends of Hitler.

My Dad had laughed and danced round our kitchen when he heard that Hitler was dead.

"Hitler's toot! Hitler's toot!" Dad had said over and over, waving the *Daily Express* with its big black headline: **HITLER TOD**

No more war. No more planes in the night. No more dark fears. Now Auntie Ena, Uncle Kenny, Mam and Dad were being friends with Hort and Gert. It was too difficult for me. Was this no more war? Was this Christmas? It must be.

The Germans began to sing in harmony, very softly and beautifully:

"Stille Nacht, heilige Nacht
Alles schlaft, einsam wacht
Nur das traute, hochheilige Paar
Holder Knabe im lockigen Haar,
Schlaf in himmlischer Ruh,
Schlaf in himmlischer Ruh."

We held our breath to listen. All was calm. All was bright.

And then my baby sister, lying on Gert's knee as he sang, wet her nappy right through her rubber pants and his grey uniform.

And everybody laughed and laughed and said it was lucky and laughed again as if they would never stop.

THE XMAS TREAT

WE used to be asked to save silver sweetie wrappers to raise money and that is what my childhood Christmases were like – shiny sweet scraps overlaid one on top of the other to make a single beautiful ball of memories.

All through my primary school years the highlight was *THE XMAS TREAT* in the village hall.. For weeks, our teacher and the visiting music teacher would coach us and rehearse us in our party pieces. There was always a concert when we entertained the grown-ups to songs and sketches before they entertained us to food and games. All ages came. The school was right at the heart of the community. There was a warm feeling of belonging to everyone and of having their interest and their care and through us the village could enjoy Christmas *'because Christmas was for the children'*. It was wonderful. The Christmas tree, donated by one of the big houses, was a frondy giant, towering to the rafters, lit by real candles clipped to the branches, with packets for everyone lying along its flat wide arms. The resiny smell, the dark mystery of it and the excitement of trying to spot one's own parcel, to guess at its contents – all wonderful.

After the concert, after the speeches, chairs were pushed back and the children were seated at trestle tables. We were all handed paper bags containing sandwiches, buns and cake. Ladies with urns and teapots poured scalding mugs of tea. Oranges were distributed and then, while the last of us was still scattering crumbs, a thunderous voice would call the village to thankfulness for mercies received – a voice I knew well – the voice of our neighbour, The Very Reverend Dr Lauchlan MacLean–Watt, ex-Moderator, ex-minister of Glasgow Cathedral and, since his last birthday, in his own words, an *octo-geranium*.

A little round ball of a man with an immense presence, he marched up and down the hall urging us to greater and greater efforts as he led us in singing, *"All people that on earth do dwell sing to the Lord with cheerful voice"*.

I still sing the Old Hundredth as if Dr Lauchlan is at my back.

Then there were games: *Grand Old Duke of York, Farmer's in His Den, Pass the Parcel, Stations,* and finally it was time for the great man himself to come striding in over the stage, ringing his bell. Not the minister, not my father but Santa Claus himself. Never any reindeer.

For several magical years I believed in him and marvelled at his coming to lowly mortals like ourselves in our wee village. Then one year I paid the price of being the headmaster's daughter. I was still there, behind the stripped tree after the other children had gone, waiting for my father who was speaking to Santa Claus himself. I was glorying in this honour being done to my Daddy when Santa hitched up his red robe to reveal a very ordinary pair of trousers and wellies and pulled out of his hip pocket a packet of Players. He groaned with weariness as he did this and the scales fell from my eyes. He was just ordinary like the man from the garage. He *was* the man from the garage, the one who worked the petrol-pumps.

I stood sick with revelation behind the tree and my innocence fell away from me.

Still, I got over it. I rationalised, as children do, that Santa must be using substitutes to save his energy for the big night. I believed what I wanted to believe. I walked home with my father that evening as happy as could be. My mother and the baby were waiting at home and I had got a boat off the tree. I did not tell Dad what I had seen.

The frosty sky was ablaze with Merry Dancers, the Northern Lights, the aurora borealis. They leaped and shimmered and streaked ahead of us and the road sparkled white at our feet. I clutched my Daddy's hand, my boat in the other, and I sang. I was six and life was just perfect. I was captain of my own ship.

STOCKING UP

ON Christmas mornings we used to bring our sacks and socks into our parents' big bed. We would climb in at the foot and cosily and delightedly pull out all the good things and share our delight.

The stockings were hung downstairs on the sitting-room mantelpiece because there was no sense in expecting Santa to come down through the Rayburn flue and out the wee door. There was no handle on the inside. It was the burning fiery furnace problem all over again but in reverse.

At first we hung up Dad's big kilt socks but as we got bigger so did the presents so we began to pin hopeful pillow-cases to the wood above the fireplace. The mantelpiece became pockmarked with pinholes. Often in the morning it was covered with sooty finger-prints; once there were sooty boot-prints all over the hearth and the linoleum. This was the clincher; Mum was annoyed. Once we found a terrific clue – some white beard, real hair, stuck in the wood of the mantelpiece and one year there was a thank-you poem for the sherry in a crabby hand which nobody recognized when I took it to school.

Our belief in a domestic Santa continued for many years. First, I conspired privately not to disillusion my little sister and then it seemed imperative to both of us that we did not disillusion my parents. We kept it going for ages. Even after we left for the Academy and our stockings held stockings and bath salts and notepaper we kept up the cosy Christmas ritual and always there would be tangerines in the toes.

Later there would be Christmas lunch – one of our own hens boiled to make broth and then eaten with tatties from the garden and tinned peas. There would be jelly and tea and Christmas cake, crackers and funny hats and underneath all the gaiety, as I grew older, I would feel sad. I always felt sad on Christmas afternoon because, try as I might, I could never get to the heart of it, to capture the atmosphere I read about in books. I would feel it slipping through my fingers and the harder I tried the less I seemed to grasp.

It was the religious aspect of Christmas that was missing on Christmas Day. It was there in school with its carols and its stories because school was open to all denominations. School had its own established practice and all was well with Christmas while we were there but at home, had my parents adhered to the dogma of the Strict Presbyterian ministers and elders there would have been no Christmas at all. The S.P.s did not countenance Christmas. With that peculiar form of double-think at which they excelled in those days, they declared Christmas to be a Popish, pagan festival and they celebrated New Year instead with whisky and black bun and a weekday church service – at exactly the same time as the annual shinty match.

Later, when my sister and I wanted to put up paper chains and Christmas cards, these had to be confined to the dining-room because an old elder spent Sabbath afternoons with us to avoid unnecessary travel between morning and evening services and it would never do for his eyes to light on our frivolity and papery Popery.

He and my father used to smoke their pipes after Sunday lunch and chat or snooze on either side of the fire while we, the women of the house, disappeared to our bedrooms to read under the covers and stay out of mischief. One wintry afternoon my father was nodding off gently when the elder let out a groan. He had been crouching over the fire and studying the mantelpiece.

"O, Seoras, Sabbath or no Sabbath I have to tell you.

"That's a terrible attack of woodworm you've got there. You'll have to do something about it. There's even some new holes since I was here last!"

SCAPEGOAT

THERE were seven of us in our primary class at Upper Drasdale and I was on top. I sat at the back of the room all the time I was in Miss MacArthur's class. Bored stiff. Except on Primary 5 when I watched and absorbed the extra tuition she gave to the boys of P7, whom she regarded as extra-special. One of them became a doctor and one a professor, special enough for a village school. The others? I don't know. Scattered all over the world, I expect.

So there we were – my class on P7 now – on a day dark with rain, desperate with terror. We were doing decimals. Miss Mac had been having a love affair. We knew this by the way we had to keep quiet while she wrote at her table behind the two easels. She wrote; we kept our heads down till the letter was licked and stamped and sent out to Malachi's mail bus in time to catch the train east.

One of us – always a boy – would get the privilege of going out and holding up the letter at the roadside. Malachi would lean out and grab the envelope without stopping, just like the guards did with the tablet on the station platform four miles away at Lochanallt.

All P7 silently vied for the privilege of getting out to post the love letter. Nothing ever came of it – the romance, I mean. She would die a spinster, but we didn't know that then. To us it was tension – the difference between a bad mood all day and maybe the belt – or peace and perhaps some poetry.

THIS day went wrong from the start. The high windows let in very little light. The 60-watt bulbs on their long flexes were of little help. They swung gently to and fro in the heat of the radiators. Nobody explained to us why they did this and we were too scared to ask, though we wondered.

We were doing decimals: *.875 of a* £1 = ? These were the days of farthings and halfpennies, rods, poles and perches, chains the length of a cricket pitch, alien things.

I had an advantage because my father, the schoolmaster, had a chain. Sometimes the crofters asked him to measure their land to help with a form and I went with him to hold the end of the chain. So I knew that a chain meant a real chain. I knew the feel of it. From that I deduced that rods and poles had similar meanings but a perch was something my budgie sat on or an English fish that you caught in storybooks.

There were these two birds sitting on a perch and the one said to the other, "Can you smell fish?"

So this day we were doing decimals. That's what Primary 7 did; heavy stuff – compound vulgar fractions, decimals, taps filling baths – Holmes Book 5.

It was dark; it was wet; there was thunder in the air. If the bus brought back any messages we didn't know about them. There was no good news for any of us that day. Her temper was foul.

The more she shouted the more frozen we became. P5 and P6 had almost stopped breathing in their attempts to be invisible. The stage was all ours: Donnie, Gordon, Lena, Iain, DJ, Fiona and me, cowering and shivering.

Nobody could think because of the vilification that had been heaped upon us. Nobody was free from it; it did not matter a bit whether we were sitting in the front row or the back

We were all morons, idiots, nincompoops. We stung and cringed under the lash of her tongue. The shadow of the belt hung over us like the gloom of the day but for some reason she stopped short of belting us .

POINT eight seven five was the sticking point. Express it as a vulgar fraction. Everybody hoped somebody else would answer and save the day. Nobody did.

I was in the back seat. I knew they were all pinning their hopes on me but I had been as stupefied by the yelling and the sarcasm as everybody else. I was like a rabbit in the headlights, weaselled, stuck.

There was a pause. A silence. Then a shriek. "Out! Out! All of you! To the headmaster's room! Go."

We were in a very small rural school but the divide between us and the headmaster was a big important examination – an examination that divided the sheep from the goats. The sheep went off on the train to Dingwall, where the mart and the Academy were. The goats stayed at home in the west. My father taught the goats until they were fifteen.

Years and years ago, when I was very small my mother had called me a goat and I had burst into tears, saying "Yes, I'm a goat. I know I'm a goat." The fact that I had gained 100 per cent in the Verbal Reasoning Test, to everyone's astonishment, made no difference at all. I still felt I was a goat.

We trailed along the corridor to the Advanced Division door. Their room was much lighter and airier than ours with windows to the north and south. Light has always lifted my spirits. Their desks were modern and shiny. I felt eased by this but not by my father that morning.

He glowered down at us from his high desk like a pillar of dark-ness but I could feel his struggle. My Dad was not like that, not really. He was better, lighter. This was the headmaster speaking, scornful, accusing, supporting his senior teacher.

What was this? We could not turn .875 into a vulgar fraction? What were we? Infants? What was wrong with us? He would ask us again; ask each one.

We hung our heads and hoped for invisibility. There were seven of us. One of us was bound to get it right. The boys guessed wildly and the girls followed suit until by a miracle my pal, Fiona hit on the right answer.

"Seven-eighths," she whispered and in a flash, seeing she was right, I echoed the magic number. Saved! We were ordered to sit down; the others were lined up, yelled at and belted. Two big double-handers each.

DJ was first and went to the back of the line nursing his palms. Fiona and I watched, shaking and guilty, from the silky honey-coloured desks, separated now from our classmates by seven-eighths.

We watched them move up one by one. I held my breath. It couldn't happen. No. It couldn't. Yes it did. My father had wound himself up into such a frenzy that he belted poor Donald John twice. And nobody had the nerve to point out his mistake, least of all DJ. We all sat there and saw that the big boss on his pedestal had feet of clay and not one of us had the courage to speak up. Back home after school the incident was not mentioned by my father or myself that night or ever again.

As we trooped dismally back to our classroom the others were in pain but I was in agony. Now I was not only apart from the class but I had to bear the burden of knowing that my father, whom I adored, had made a terrible mistake, a very public error.

Any time I hear anybody of my generation say they were belted and it did them no harm I think of 0.875, as it became known later, and I wish – oh, I wish – that I had been belted that day along with the others.

THREE years later I was a boarder at the County Secondary School, enjoying Academy life but missing my home. West-coast girls had to go back to the Girls' Hostel for lunch while hostel boys were fed in the school canteen like the town pupils, an arrangement we detested.

It was a wintry March. We had chilblains and runny noses and it was the day of the Latin exam. With sausage stew and semolina inside and slushy snow outside, we tramped back to school, muttering declensions.

Our road ran downhill through old parkland overgrown with rhododendrons. The boys were waiting for us. They had laid an ambush in the bushes. Squeals, shrieks, yells and snowballs filled the air. Boy leaped upon girl, rubbing snow into cheeks already bright with cold. Girls ran or retaliated. Wet, gasping and exhilarated, the melée whirled towards the school gates.

Nobody noticed that I had been singled out. Willie MacFee was of a tinker family that spent its summers round Lochanallt and the winter in town. He had always been an unwilling pupil in my father's class and was just marking time till he reached fifteen and could leave school altogether. His snowball had a rock in it. It hit me square on the temple and knocked me to the ground.

"That's for what your father did to me!" he snarled, jumping on me and thumping me a few more times just for effect. Then he vanished.

Head ringing, I staggered to my feet and followed the crowd. The electric bell was shrilling and its imperative could not be denied. A bedraggled crew, we hung up our wet coats and with dripping hair and stinging cheeks went in to our exam.

I looked at the paper; it seemed to be all right. My head felt strange and hot but I could do the translations. I usually got most of it right. It was a bit like the Verbal Reasoning Test on P7. I wrote swiftly and then put my head on the desk and fell asleep.

The Latin teacher came up the aisle and patted my head.

"Craitur!" he said.

I roused myself and in a panic looked at what I had done. It was rubbish! Gobbledy-gook. I tried again; did the whole exam again, wrote feverishly and finished just in time. I felt strange and dull and sleepy.

"Are you all right, craitur?" the Latin teacher asked again.

"I'm fine." I said. "Fine."

I told nobody about Willie MacFee. Not a living soul, not even my best pal, Fiona. I felt I owed him that. After all, the Ten Commandments had been dinned into us in primary school: "*Visiting the iniquities of the fathers upon the children* ... " That was all it was, wasn't it?

Rough justice.

INNER SOUND

THE juicy langour of a school afternoon, dreamy, smelling of cut grass and wet boys. A thick shaft of dusty sunlight across the wooden floor. The teacher's pointer smacks the cracked oilskin map.

"The Inner Hebrides; the Outer Hebrides.

Repeat after me. . . The Inner Hebrides: Raasay. Skye. The Small Isles. Mull. . ."

Soporific chanting: "Raasay, Skye, the small isles, mull...."

"The Outer Hebrides: Lewis, Harris; North Uist, Benbecula; South Uist, Barra."

"Lewis Harris, North Uist ...

South Uist...

Joey sits in the back seat, mind wandering: *Inner Hebrides, Outer Hebrides... The Shorter Catechism, the Longer Catechism...*

Easter Ross; Wester Ross – that's us, pink on the map like the British Empire.

Wester Ross = Bester Ross; Easter Ross = Leaster Ross...

*Easter holidays; Wester holidays ... no that doesn't work ... it would though,
if you lived in Aberdeen. Norther; souther ...no that doesn't work. Northerly/
southerly – aha! Blow the wind southerly. Northern lights. Southern lights?
I don't know.*

Where now? What else?

Upper Drasdale; Lower Drasdale yes, that's us:

Upper Drasdale, Wester Ross,

(Opposite the Inner Hebrides)

Scotland.

Great Britain,

Europe,

The World,

The Universe. . . .

*Uncle Dougal in Wokingham, Bucks, England, puts N.B. on his letters to
Dad just to annoy him.*

N.B. = North Britain.

*That makes England = S.B. = South Britain. I wanted Dad to put S.B. on
his letters to Uncle Dougal but he said that was too rude.*

Why? Why is N.B. not too rude too?

OOPS!

CRACK! The pointer whacks the desk.

"Yes, miss. No, miss. Please, miss, I *was* listening. Yes, miss. I know,
miss. Off Raasay? The sea off Raasay?

It's the Inner Sound, Miss."

SAVED

I WAS thirteen when Billy Graham came to the Town Hall – not in the flesh, just his disembodied voice:

> *Softly and tenderly Jesus is calling*
> *Calling for you and for me*
> *See at the portals he's waiting and watching*
> *Watching for you and for me.*

I was a boarder in the Girls' Hostel, a castle up on the hill. It's quite posh now – a hotel and conference centre – but in the fifties it was like Colditz. Seventy girls were interned there from half past five at night until school next morning. Cold stone floors, bare windows, wooden benches, plain fare.

It was more spartan than any convent. We were expected to live a lifestyle that made the Poor Clares look like hedonists.

41

Shutters were put on the windows so that we could not look out for – *whisper it* – ʙᴏʏs – and the whole castle would lie festering with boredom on lovely Sunday afternoons, swapping *True Romances* for the *Roxy* or the *Valentine*, thick-headed with boredom and oxygen starvation.

The only exceptions were the Strict Presbyterians. After lunch we put on our Kangols and tramped yet again down to the tin tabernacle in the town to receive the undiluted milk of the pure gospel from the minister's intended. It was monotonous but at least we were well-exercised in our bodies as well as in the Shorter Catechism.

And now and again on our pilgrimages we would catch a glimpse of a wandering boy. Or even a man!

We were very rarely allowed out in the evenings and when we were it was by dint of pleading and wheedling and getting the matron in a good mood. And it could only be to something very worthy, so when the Billy Graham relay came to the Town Hall everybody went. It was a night out.

I was not in the least interested in more religion. I got enough of it on Sundays but it was a jaunt. There was always the chance we might get to Morganti's for chips and we were not obliged to wear a hat. In fact, it seemed so frivolous by comparison to the grim services of the S.P.s that it did not seem like proper religion at all.

The Town Hall wasn't a church, for one thing. There were potted plants all along the stage, just like at the Mod and groups of counsellors in tight blue suits stood about with sincere but cheerful expressions on their faces, waiting and watching.

It all seemed quite harmless until the relay began and then it was horrible.

Every minute of it was horrible. Horrible to be trapped in a seat with that voice coming at you over the loudspeaker, working into you, beating at your mind, wheedling, cajoling, stealing your soul. It was the new insidious voice of advertising, the American soft-sell.

Every once in a while the organ would break out into sugar-coated choruses and everyone would sing, all cosy and friendly.

It was like having a bath in warm syrup, so easy to relax into and drift.

Then the exhortations started for sinners to come forward and give themselves up.

Surrender to Jesus.... just as you are.... come forward now.... come, come... come home. poor sinner, come home"

I stared at my socks and wished it would end. Glared at my socks and willed it to end. This was worse than a hundred unwilling Sabbaths in the S.P. Church. I could not see that anyone would be daft enough to respond to such shallow soft-soapery.

But then the shuffling started – the creaking and sniffing and quiet shuffling. I took a quick look round and could not believe my eyes. The bench in front of me was deserted. Vacant. Bare. All the Hostel boys who had been there, including Jock Chisholm, the biggest reprobate in 2B, were pushing forward, emotionally wrecked.

I was stunned. I went to nudge my pal to share my surprise and amusement but my elbow hit empty air. Everybody in our row was making for the front. I was completely on my own. Panic-stricken, I looked about me. The passages were now as clogged as a fank at the dipping; there was nobody left in the seats that I knew – indeed, there was hardly anybody left at all. I bowed my head to hide my confusion, afraid to catch anyone's eye. What was wrong with me? Why was I different? What had the others heard that I hadn't? I could not believe that this was happening. It was like a nightmare.

The music crescendoed in triumph. The fish had been netted, the sheep gathered in. One last deeply sincere summons to surrender and then the doors opened on outer darkness. The goats had had their chance. They were free to go.

It was a lonely road home through the empty streets and up the long steep hill but I could not get away fast enough and I had absolutely no thought of waiting until the others had completed their initiation. I carried a lonely burden of sin and self-will and sheer pig-headed independent thinking.

It was even darker through the Lodge gates into the derelict park and up the unlit drive where snaky rhododendrons crept close and branches creaked overhead. But I was not alone I discovered. I had a God. I wasn't sure about him yet but he was there despite the boredom of church and its meaningless sermons.

Past the spooky tree-stump I chanted to ward off the lurking panic:

'Yea, though I walk in death's dark vale
Yet shall I fear none ill
For Thou art with me, and Thy rod
And staff me comfort still

What I was sure about was that He was a stern and gritty God, tough and resilient, not that sugar-coated saviour on offer in the Town Hall.

At last I reached the light and the big outside door and I was back.

Alone I went to the dining-room where mugs of milk and buns and marge awaited. For once I did not have to grab and push to get an uncracked mug.

The matron appeared. "Are you on your own, child? Where are the others?"

I wiped off my moustache and stared at her solemnly. Mrs Mac was a formidable woman with an iron-grey bun and a very unbecoming clingy knitted dress. A silk scarf was always twisted round her dew-laps and pinned with a Celtic silver brooch. She stared at me sternly.

"Saved. They've all been saved. Except me."

Mrs Mac's face twisted.

"And what about you? Didn't *you* want to be saved ?"

"No. When they all went down the front I just stayed where I was and then I came back."

"Well, well. Off you go now and have a bath before the others come. There's plenty of hot water."

A bath was a luxury only permitted once a week on strict rota. Maybe my goat smell was too much for Mrs Mac or maybe it was a reward for free-thinking. You never knew where you were with her.

When the born-again came trooping into the dorm, I was tucked up, cosy for once in my army camp-bed, sheltering behind a John Buchan thriller. There was a sudden hush when they observed me and then they began talking among themselves in high excited voices while they got into their pyjamas.

Just before lights-out they all knelt down and prayed. Nothing like this had ever happened before. We had all been collectively terrified of the pious and holy-oly but here they all were praying aloud and in turn – all twenty of them. And worse! They were praying for me without my permission, that I would be saved soon. I was outraged.

Behind the John Buchan I sent up counter-signals, interceptor missiles to cancel them out.

"Please, God, don't let me be converted yet. I don't want to be saved. Not yet. I want to go and see Gregory Peck in *Roman Holiday* next Saturday afternoon. Please, God, don't let me be saved before then."

I wasn't.

MRS CAMERON

BELLA Cameron was the wife of the bus driver in the small West Coast village of Arnaig. They had no children and neither did her twin sister who lived east in the Black Isle and thought herself a cut above Bella because she had married a missionary, a lay preacher in the Strict Presbyterians.

Cameron was a man who liked a dram and a joke and who didn't bother too much with religion except to put on a clean collar on the Sabbath and take a turn to the meeting-house just often enough to keep the elders off his back.

They were in their fifties, both of them, when Bella got the *cùram*, the change, spiritual as well as physical. She saw the light. Like Paul on the road to Damascus, Christ spoke to her and her whole world changed. Poor Cameron now had a religious wife; one who had renounced all worldly things; one who lived for nothing but worship and prayer and solemn church-going.

Bella had always dressed sombrely. She had the tall, spare elegance of good highland blood: strong fine bones and pure silver hair swept up in a roll. Black suited her. She wore long skirts and short jackets and a small black hat. Peasant that she was, she could have passed for a duchess. She had style, which her identical twin lacked for all her fur-coated finery.

The Strict Presbyterians had broken away from the Free Kirk on a point of doctrine at the end of the 19th century. They were a sect of the North-west Highlands though many of the bigger cities had a church and a minister to cater for the Highland diaspora. Ministers were in short supply and many congregations had to make do with untrained elders and missionaries, who made up in fervour what they lacked in education.

Each congregation held a communion season twice a year, a holiday which lasted from so-called Fast Day on Thursday right through the weekend till lunchtime on Monday.

Hospitality was given freely to all-comers and it was a matter of pride, after the long, long Sabbath sitting, for the man of the house to bring home as many as he could to share the Scotch broth and the mutton and tatties his wife had so carefully prepared the night before. Afterwards there would be trifle or jelly whipped up with Carnation milk, then tea and a smoke by the fireside before evening service began. Ministers were discussed, sermons dissected. It was a religious folkfest and for most people such concentrated over-indulgence twice a year was quite enough to satisfy them.

But for the saved, the elect, this was not the case. It was their mission to hunger for Christ, to feed off the milk of the pure gospel, to partake of the bread and the wine as often as they could. Once their piety was proved and they had received the communion token, an actual coin, relic of the days when the Westminster Confession of Faith was a radical document, they were in the inner circle.

To achieve this status was never easy. Not only had you to overcome your own sense of unworthiness, miserable sinner and worm of the dust that you were; not only had you to overcome the guilt and the shame dinned into you from the pulpit from early childhood, but you then had to convince the elders of the tribe that you were worthy.

Little wonder that the greater percentage of any highland congregation sat still when the beloved of Christ were summoned to share his supper. They had all just listened to a fire and brimstone half-hour called *Fencing the Tables*, where a visiting preacher had listed with relish all the heinous sins that debarred you from taking communion. The fornicators, the philanderers, the frivolous followers of fashion, the vainsong and the dance, the drinking and debauchery – in short, anything that smelled slightly of worldly pleasure debarred you from the Lord's Table. It was a high, daunting barrier to climb and, depending on the power of the preacher, it was electrically charged.

Many folk, like Duncan Cameron, knowing full well they were among the goats for all eternity, sat back and enjoyed the performance, letting it all roll over their heads. But the sheep, the elect, often had to drag themselves, sobbing under the burden of their presumption, to partake of the chalice and the little cube of *Mother's Pride*, sanctified for the occasion and set apart from all common use.

For the elect twice a year was not enough. It was a mark of holiness to try to attend as many communion seasons as possible. Few women were able to travel but some widows and superannuated spinsters with no ties to keep them at home were regular attenders. It was all in the nature of a pilgrimage, a hark back to the *Turas*, the holy travelling of the Celtic Church, which even the Strict Presbyterians acknowledged in their spiritual ancestry.

BELLA Cameron took to the road. She became a pilgrim. Carrying only her old leather handbag and her Bible, defended only by her faith, she travelled the country on foot in all weathers.

At first she did not go far. Taking lifts where she could get them, accepting hospitality where it was offered, she visited the neighbouring villages, then gradually ventured further and further afield.

The community of the Strict Presbyterians was tight. Everyone knew everyone else so she built up a network of homely houses, doorsteps where she was welcomed. Highland hospitality was still a strong force. The roads were full of tramps and travelling people after two world wars. Tea and a scone were freely given and often a shilling for a smoke as well.

But Mrs Cameron was no tramp. Nor was she a beggar. She only ever needed a cup of tea and a piece of bread and butter and a room in which to pray for a while. She kept her dignity and her style. The weather freshened her fine skin to a rain-washed pink; her clothes were shabby but they suited her. Her sister, however, disowned her. That was one door where there was no welcome, one meeting-house she avoided.

At first, she went home to Duncan after each sortie, refreshed and ready to settle for a while, but gradually the addiction grew. She took off from one communion to another without touching base and that was when the trouble started.

Elders began to mutter; questions were asked at session meetings. The gospels according to Paul were consulted.

At the next communion her token was withdrawn. She was unworthy. She had left her husband. Technically no separation had taken place because she had just wandered off and forgotten to come back. She lived now on a different plane.

Duncan did not mind. It was a relief when she was away; he had peace from her everlasting psalm-singing and prayers morning, noon and night. He could drop in on the pub with an easy conscience.

But the church would not have it. What God had joined let no man put asunder and even if the Man had lived 2,000 years before and was the Son of God Himself, that was not a sufficient reason. She was judged and condemned and her punishment was terrible. They banned her from communion and told her she would get her token back only if she went home to Arnaig and became a wife again. So she went, humbly and submissively and took up where life there had left off. And that seemed to be the end of that.

Time passed. Bella got her communion token back once she had proved herself. The talk subsided. People forgot.

But the pent-up forces of Bella's quiet passion had to find an outlet. It was spring-cleaning time. Bella went over to the shop in Arnaig and bought some green paint. She painted the doors, the windows, the mirrors and the cups. She painted the floor and the kettle. All green. She even painted her good black shoes.

Then she took up her hat and her handbag and hit the road once more.

Our house in the next village was one of her favoured stops. My mother was always kind to people of the road and Mrs Cameron was a special favourite.

"Och, the poor soul!" My mother would say. "People are so unkind. I don't believe the half of it. Green paint indeed!"

But my sister and I had heard the fantastical gossip too and we wanted to be sure. We hid behind the door to peep for paint. Mrs Cameron was her usual stately self in her usual threadbare black. But our beady sensation-seeking eyes had found the proof we craved.

On her dusty black shoes there were still a few faint spots of green.

We clutched each other in the shadows, excited by the revelation and were thoroughly scolded by my mother and sent to make the tea.

TIME passed. Mrs Cameron went on her way and I went on mine to Edinburgh University. All through my childhood I had promised myself that as soon as I could I would escape from the thunderous boredom of the S.P. Kirk but, just to please my father, whom I adored, I went to the Edinburgh S.P communion during my first weeks as a student there.

The gloomy inner city church was packed. I had never been in a church so big. I sat crushed and overwhelmed in the inside of a pew, condemned to four or five hours of boredom and wishing I had never come. At least five ministers were presiding which meant that each had to have their say. It would be a long sederunt.

The temperature was rising but I sat in a dwalm born of long practice, away in a world of my own. The condemnations in Galatians Chapter 5 roared over my head unheeded, the wheedling encouragement to the elect had nothing to do with me. And then the communicants began to creep forward to the communion table, a real table at the front of the pews.

It could not hold them all at once so there would be several sittings each with a different minister presiding.

The first sitting was served. I yawned. We started all over again. The second sitting. The third.

AND then the uproar began.

I sat bolt upright, shocked. Mrs Cameron was being debarred from the Lord's Table! Sobbing and crying, she was dragged bodily up the aisle by two burly elders, others following in a solid phalanx. Here in this strange city a woman of my own country was being assaulted and abused in a public place in full view of hundreds of people and nobody was lifting a hand to help her.

She was offering passive resistance, something that was not then as familiar as it is now. They were hauling her along the passage between the shocked faces, her skirt above her knees, her hat hanging on by one pin, her long white hair tumbling over her face.

I trampled feet all along the pew, shoving past fat knees, sweeping Bibles off the bookboard as I went, ignoring the protests and yelps of pain.

"Stop it! Stop that! Are you mad?" I screamed. "Would Christ have treated a woman like this? Read your Bibles, you hypocrites! Judge not that ye be not judged!"

Hands reached out to grab me too but I punched them aside. I was enormous in my anger, red-faced and powerful. The elders shrank back. The ministers fell silent. The congregation was agape.

"Mrs Cameron, a ghràidh," I said gently, helping her up and straightening her clothes. "Come away. Come away from here. Come home with me." And with my arm around her shoulders we turned our backs on them and walked out of the silent church.

IF only it could have been that way. If only. In my daydreams I have relived that scenario again and again, especially as I have reached the age Bella Cameron was then. If only I had had the nerve to do what I felt. But I was too young, too insecure, too hemmed in to challenge authority like that. In reality all I did was watch in horror and pity and anger while the only person I recognised in that whole multitude was manhandled to the back of the church and dumped sobbing in a pew, while the self-righteous elders, their duty done, tramped back to continue the charade of eating and drinking in Christ's name.

That was the end of the S.P.s as far as I was concerned. I wrote to my father that afternoon, in itself a transgression of the Lord's Day, and I told him I was never going back.

"You'd better accept it, Murdo." my mother said. "You've lost her, as far as the Church is concerned." And my father knew when to leave well alone. He never mentioned church attendance to me again.

BELLA Cameron continued to walk the roads, to call at houses, to pray behind dykes and to sleep who knows where. I lost contact with the West Coast for many years because my father took a job on the east side of the county in the parish of the very church where Bella's sister still queened it sleekly in her fur coat.

The scandal at the city church had shocked more than me and as the years went by the judgemental dogma mellowed somewhat. Bella's burning zeal and total commitment to her faith, manic though it was, had to be acknowledged and respected. Nobody tried to restrain her again, neither in home or church or institution and her pilgrimage continued right into her seventies until she died one starry night at prayer by the roadside.

Her *turas* had come full circle.

ORANGE AND BLUES

MACDERMOTT was in the refectory, peeling an orange. The pungent Cointreau smell filled the space between us and my nose twitched. I could feel a sneeze coming on."It's not as if we could do anything about it."

Too depressed to reply, I watched his hands. His peeling of the orange was global. First he scored lines round the Arctic and Antarctic circles, then down the lines of longitude. Zest pinged out, pricking my nostrils.

"You see, you have to apply different standards to these folk," he went on.

The clasp knife he was using was clotted with filth where the handle met the haft. I imagined the pockets of his vast tweed overcoat silted with fluff and tobacco shreds and old encrusted caramels and I turned from the thought in disgust.

He had begun to remove the skin. Bright shards fell on the formica.

His thumbnail was cracked and ridged, the quick packed with dirt.

He inserted it around Iceland and stripped the rind down to the Equator, exposing the bulging, naked pith.

"And anyway, it's all happening so far away."

The whole Atlantic Ocean down to the Falklands was revealed.

The sneeze that had been building up at the back of my nose suddenly burst out, taking me by surprise. The air between us was a battleground, bacteria versus citronella. I drew back, blowing hard into a Kleenex.

MacDermott paid no attention. His thumb ripped off Scandinavia and half of Siberia.

"After all, it's not as if we know all the facts."

Russia, Afghanistan and the Indian sub-continent fell, curled, to the table-top.

"We only get what's fed to us by the media and who decides that anyway?"

He was speaking quickly now, flaying the globe mercilessly. In one swift stroke he had stripped the Americas north to south and the whole sphere lay defenceless in his horny fist. I waited for him to crush it, dripping on to the bare plastic but instead he began to pick fastidiously at the white pith, paring it off gently so as not to break the membrane underneath.

"It's not as if we can do anything about it. We do have our own lives to lead."

The orange was completely naked now. I felt tense. Consummation was at hand. He folded up the clasp-knife by bending the blade against his knee. I had a sudden vision of him catching the top of his thumb as the hinge snapped shut and for an instant my blood turned white.

He dropped the knife into his overcoat and looked at me earnestly.

"Time enough when it actually happens, eh?"

His thumb plunged into the tender orifice at the North Pole and he wrenched the fruit apart. Membranes tore and juices spurted.

My eyes were watering now and my nose ran incessantly. I pinched my nostrils shut with my one damp Kleenex.

"I'm telling you their birth rate's too high as it is."

His mouth under the tobacco-stained moustache was pursed with the intensity of his concentration. He lifted one of the juicy quadrants to his face. His mouth opened.

"It doesn't do to think about it too much. Besides, it could never happen here."

He inserted the segment and chewed noisily. His face screwed up and he swallowed.

"Ach! This orange is no use. It's sour. Would you like a bit?"

I shook my head. He picked up the rejected fragments of his ruined globe and dumped them in the ashtray among the fag ends and the sweetie papers.

"Well, I must be off. It was nice meeting you. It does you good to have a real heart-to-heart with a kindred spirit now and then."

LANDSCAPE WITH SHEEP

"W HAT'S the hurry, lassie?" The voice came from behind a cluster of boats pulled up above the high-water mark.

"Oh, Alick! There you are. Help me get the boat out. Dad's sheep are on the saltings. They'll be stranded for sure."

"Where's your father that he's not with you? You can't do much on your own. "

"They're all away at Inverness for the day. I saw the sheep go down the shore but I didn't think they'd get so far round. Come *on*, Alick."

Alick was our next-door neighbour and my favourite *bodach*. He had known me since I was in my pram. He knew plenty about sheep. He knew how they liked to get down on the saltings to crop the short salty turf. He knew the dangers. They would wander along, heads down, munching, never heeding the encroaching sea until they were marooned. Then they would just stand there and drown like the Solway martyrs.

"Ach! I've no time for sheep, horrible voracious brutes! The curse

56

of the Highlands. Everything subjugated to them, houses burned over people's heads for them, hillsides burned to grow grass for them."

And here I was, near killing myself, rushing to their rescue. It wasn't so much that I cared for sheep but that I didn't care for what my father would say when he came home to find that I had let his sheep commit suicide.

"Oh, Alick. Hurry up! *Please*." I was dancing with impatience.

The saltings at the head of the loch were well covered now. The spring tide was nosing up the channels between the succulent tussocks, joining up, making islands, deepening and widening all the time.

What was that poem about *the cruel crawling foam*? *Oh Mary, go and call the cattle home . . .* that was it. She'd been no better at keeping an eye on beasts than I was.

Alick put away the net he was mending as methodically as if he had belonged to the Royal Guild of Needlewomen and came stumping in his wellies over the boulders and knotgrass to our boat.

I had thrown my sandals into the bow and lined up the rollers so that we were all set to haul her down to the water. Every minute made the distance shorter. The tide was lapping the first of my rollers already.

"Ho hup!" called Alick. Gripping the gunwale and facing each other, we heaved the boat out of the sand and on to the logs. Once she was afloat, I snatched up the rollers and flung them onto the grass, then splashed through the little wavelets to push the boat out.

Alick was already in the stern letting his weight help the boat into deeper water. He poled with his oar and I pushed then scrambled over the stem. We were clear. Alick took the starboard oar and I took the other, pulling steadily, bare feet propped on the thwart in front of me.

I love these spring tides when the loch is a big see-through mirror. You can slide across the glassy surface, dark with reflected mountains and peer down to the roots of the seaweed forests where whelks are pursuing their whelky business, leaving winding trails in the slake.

But no time for that tonight! Alick and I fairly ploughed through the water. Sheep are awkward enough brutes to shift, but wet sheep are the very devil.

The seaweed was breaking the surface now. My oar was making little whirlpools. Soon our keel was dunting softly over turf, over the drowned seapinks, silver bubbles trapped in their leaves. We stood up and poled the boat along, fending it off the shallows and trying to follow the maze of deeper channels, black with rotten seaweed.

The sheep were huddled on the last remaining islets, three of them on one and one on the other.

"Keep the boat steady, girl," said Alick, splashing over the gunwale. The sheep stirred uneasily at his approach but stuck to their green island, baaing stupidly.

Alick didn't waste a movement. He grasped a sheep by the scruff and the rump and swung it into the well of the boat. It wailed at the indignity, feet skittering on the bottom boards.

The next one tried to jump out but I leaned the oar on its back and held it down. It subsided and they huddled miserably together, scattering droppings among the fish scales.

The third sheep tried to get away from Alick and floundered off into shallow water. Swearing in fluent Gaelic, Alick threshed after it. He got a grip on the brute and hauled it, dripping, to the side of the boat. The water had made it a dead weight and it needed the two of us to heave it over the gunwale. It fell on its back, frightening the others and for a minute I thought we were going to capsize.

There was no room for the fourth sheep. I was just about to open my mouth to point this out when Alick let out a yell.

"Oh! *Gonadh ort*! Why could you not tell me the tide was coming in?"

"What?" I said, thinking he had gone daft. What were we doing here if the tide was not coming in? And then I realised. He had been too involved to notice the water was lapping his boot tops until it had slopped inside.

Poor Alick! I burst out laughing. "Take them off like me," I said.

"And let you see my corns! No fear! I'll keep my feet to myself. It's not decent the way you go about with these naked toes, girl!"

"Maybe you'd better keep them on. We don't want to gas the sheep, do we? "

Relief was making me cheeky.

"Ach, *isd thu*! We'd better be getting these brutes back to dry land. We still have to come back for the other one."

I suddenly came to my senses.

"Ach, Alick, I'm really sorry to have given you all this bother."

"No bother, lassie. What are neighbours for? You'll do the same for me one day. Now, *greas ort*! Get that oar going."

We propelled the boat stern-first over the turf, the seapinks deep-drowned now full fathom five. Grace Darling bringing in the ship-wrecked mariners.

Softly glide we along, softly chant we our song, I began to croon to myself: dead kings to Inchkenneth; live sheep to Kinloch. The trouble with me was my head was full of poetry and books. If it had not been away in the clouds I would have noticed the sheep straying on to the saltings in time. But then I would not have had this experience of rescuing them and it was good. It was rich. I was happy.

I turned to look at Alick's whiskery face.

"Hey, Alick, are you happy?"

"Eh?" He stared at me in disbelief. "Happy? With my seaboots full of water, my tobacco on the shore and me stinking of sheep and needing my tea. You ask me if I'm happy? *Chaneil thu glic, a bhrònag!*"

"But look at all this," I said, indicating the evening colours on the still loch. "Doesn't it make you feel good to be alive in spite of your wellies?"

Alick's eyes twinkled at me from under his fore and aft.

"I'd be a lot happier if the clegs weren't so plentiful."

We grounded on the shingle and heaved the sheep overboard. They splashed through the water and bolted up the shore, bleating and miserable. They wouldn't rest until the whole common grazing had heard of their misadventure.

Back we went for the fourth straggler. The elation had died in me. The novelty had worn off. This one was not going to be easy. The poor brute looked resigned to its fate; the tide was up past its belly and its fleece was trailing in the water. We could not see how we could lift it on board.

"There's nothing for it," said Alick. "We'll have to force it to swim."

"Ach, don't be daft, Alick. Sheep can't swim."

"Of course they can swim. They just don't know they can."

"But how?"

"We'll shove it along and keep going until we get to drier land over there where the *morach* begins.

"I'll row the boat and you'll shove the sheep."

I could not see this working but I had no better plan to offer so we brought the boat against the sheep and nudged it into deeper water. It gave a piteous wail, floundered off the submerged tussock and sank.

"Oh, Alick! We've killed it!"

"Not a bit of it. Grab it when it comes up. Get a good grip on it and I'll pull as hard as I can on the oars. Once we get it moving it'll begin to kick with its feet."

I didn't believe this but I hooked my leg under the seat, leaned over and grabbed a fistful of waterlogged fleece. The sheep's head broke the surface. Wallowing and calling, it struggled against me. I hung on for dear life.

"Come on, Alick. Pull. I can't hang on for long."

The sheep began to kick, wildly at first and then in a rhythm.

"Hey, it's swimming! Will I let go?"

"No fear. It'll not manage on its own yet."

My arms felt as if they were leaving their sockets. There was a red-hot knife twisting in my right shoulder blade.

"Pull, Alick! *Pull!*" My head was hanging down near the sheep. Its wild eyes stared into mine. I had a burst of compassion for it.

"Poor brute, never mind. We're nearly there," I told it silently.

The oars were beginning to hit bottom. The boat was bumping the turf. I was so determined to see the sheep safely ashore that I jumped overboard, skidded on the slimy grass and sat down to my armpits in the water.

Alick let out a hoot of laughter. The sheep shot away from me and made for the shore and I just sat there grinning.

Honours were even. The rescue was complete.

BONNIE GEORGE CAMPBELL

High upon Hielands and laigh upon Tay
Bonnie George Campbell rade oot on a day
Saddled and bridled sae gallant and free
Hame cam his guid horse but never cam he.
                                    *- **Traditional***

"EAT your egg, Dave," Marnie commanded. The wee boy looked disgusted.

"Pass the sugar, please, Marnie," said her mother.

"Mam, can I wear my red T-shirt?"

"No, Davy, it's in the washing-basket. I'll do it tonight."

Breakfast struggled on stickily.

Still, Marnie reflected, *we are having it at the table. It's a bit more civilised than the usual scramble. We even have a spoon in the marmalade! I do miss my book though. Conversation at this hour is a strain.*

Her parents were over for a visit while Roddie was away on a photo-graphic assignment. It was lovely to see them but hard work too.

Just then Radio Scotland, which had been blethering away in the background, sharpened its tone for the news. An item which fell on a lull in the breakfast clatter reached her, pierced her, stopped her in her life dead short:

"George Campbell, aged thirty-six, from East Kilbride, was killed yesterday evening when the car in which he was travelling hit a lamp-post on the Glasgow to Eaglesham Road. There were no other casualties."

The family noise receded into unimportance. She was stabbed with grief.

George Campbell dead.

George Campbell with his lovely gentle smile. NO! It can't be true! It couldn't be true. But it could though. He had lived in East Kilbride. He was thirty-six.

Reason told her that there were probably plenty George Campbells in the West of Scotland but instinct made her grieve for his loss. Her mind flashed back to their days together in Edinburgh.

It WAS a glorious summer afternoon. Maroon buses rumbled past, warm colour against the grey shabbiness of Nicolson Square. Hand in hand they came running and skipping down the cool canyon of shadow from the History Reading Room, brimming with light-heartedness. The world was full, shaken down and running over with delight, with youth, with effervescence, and their linked hands carried the electricity that lit up their faces.

They were on the run from eleventh-hour swotting for final exams. They were trying hard to discipline themselves to work but their passion for each other was a serious distraction. If they used different reading rooms their bodies ached for a sight of each other. If they sat together their nearness ruined concentration. Some of their elation now came from the relief of giving up the struggle for a little while.

Laughing, they collapsed on to a municipal bench in the sunshine outside Surgeons' Hall. The buses lumbered past, carrying blank faces to Trinity and Goldenacre and Fairmilehead. It was bliss to sit soaking up the sun after the dim old reading-room, saying nothing, just being together. Soon they would have to go back but life was here and now to grasp and hold forever...

"Aw, hen, move up and let us auld yins have a seat. Youse young yins have good strong legs. You shouldnae be taking up room from us poor auld craiturs."

A fierce wee wifie with a chiffon scarf over her rollers was blocking out the sunlight. Their bubble of joy reached out to her too. Willingly they cuddled up closer. She sat down, putting her oilskin bag between swollen ankles.

"Here's Jimmie," she said. "Here, Jimmie, you'll no get a seat the day. Thae students have pinched your place."

"Aw hey! No." said the decrepit wee man who had shuffled up. They all squashed closer still.

"Do you all have your special seats here?" George asked.

"Aye, right, son. You've got Jimmie's seat and he's in Jessie Murdoch's place. She'll be along in a minute."

He squeezed Marnie's hand. "Come on,he said softly. "We'll have to book tickets next time."

They stood up, laughing. "Here are your seats. We'll not stay where we're not wanted. We had no idea they belonged to you."

"Aye, son. That's right." The old ones nodded.

The two young yins ran off laughing past the bus stop and the bored queue.

IT was late, late at night. They had the flat all to themselves. The only light came from the electric fire. George and Marnie were curled up on the sagging dusty sofa, sleepy, sensuous and stroking, always stroking each other. She was nearly purring.

"Big cat," he murmured," in his soft Lewis accent. She rubbed her finger up and down the bit of hair beside his ear.

It was wonderful being with George, she thought. He took his time. He was the most seductive person she had ever met because he had patience and gentleness. He did not assault or demand. He did not try to rush her into bed and she respected him for it. He was a true gentle man.

In her circle in the early sixties, permissiveness had not yet arrived to any great degree. People did not sleep around but still there was a double standard. Boys tried all the time to see how far they could go; girls applied the sanctions. It was jungle warfare – the hunter and the hunted. The girl who gave in too easily was despised and criticised – and so was the one who was not attractive. It was wearisome. Many a virgin fell because she simply got sick of the struggle.

George Campbell did not conform to any pattern. He played his own game and for the first time ever she could relax with a man and discover her own sensuality without feeling the brakes would have to be applied any minute. He was utterly trustworthy. *Bonnie George Campbell.*

She snuggled sleepily closer. It was very late.

"Don't go home tonight, George," she said suddenly. "I can't bear to think of you trailing home in the cold. You can have Kate's bed."

It was the sort of thing she could not have offered anyone else. Kate shared a room with her.

Looking back, it seemed incredible that they could have gone to separate beds, aroused as they were, but their relationship had a strange perfect quality all of its own and their time was not yet ripe.

They went to bed, both extremely weary and relieved at the solution, George delighted at being spared the long trudge home through the rainy streets, Marnie at the novelty of the situation.

SITTING at breakfast fifteen years later, it seemed incredible to her that they had not shared a bed that night and out of her grief for him she suddenly wished with all her body and mind that they had.

"Mam, can I have another piece?"

Like a stranger she came back to them, gazing at her family in astonishment.

She had been travelling deep in past time but only a few moments had passed. She buttered a slice of toast and passed it to Davy, the sense of loss rushing over her again. Guilt tarnished her grief.

Does anyone ever grieve without feeling guilty? she wondered. *If only I had not been so stupid. If only I had behaved better things might have been so very different. What a fool I was! I had a genius for making a mess of things.*

THE night she first met George the strange little gatehouse in the cobbled cul de sac was pulsing with noise. The Lewis nurses were having a party. That afternoon Marnie had finally broken off two years of thrall to a fellow she had grown to despise but who had refused to let her go. She had seemed as powerless to cut loose as a fly in a cobweb but finally that afternoon the thread had snapped.

She was free.

She could hardly believe it yet. She was at the party alone and Duncan was a thing of the past.

She wandered from room to room, greeting someone here, talking for a while there, eating and drinking just as she pleased. Most people had come with a partner but she could do what she liked, sing or flirt or dance without the mad drunken jealousy of Duncan turning the night acidic.

As the evening grew late couples drew closer. Bodies bundled up in the heaped coats on the beds. The corners were full of whispering. Lonely now, she drifted down to the cellar of the queer wee house. Here there was dancing to smoochy music and sofas cosy with cuddles.

George Campbell was sitting alone. He caught her eye, smiled, held out his arms and she went to him, homed in on him; he was her sanctuary and she was enclosed.

"I've been waiting for you," he said. "I thought you would never come."

"IS something the matter?" her mother said sharply. "You look very queer."

Words choked in her throat. She stared at the congealed bacon on her plate, the fat turning white with cold. Disgusted, she pushed it aside and to her horror felt tears stinging her eyes. She felt sick.

All she wanted to do was to run and hide and cry but they were all looking at her and she had to say something.

"It's all right. It's just that I heard a piece of bad news on the radio just now."

"When? What news?" Sharp questions.

"It's just a fellow I used to know. He's been killed in a car crash. It was on the news just now. I got a shock."

"You must have known him very well to get in a state like that. Who was he? Was he a boyfriend?"

"George Campbell. Yes. I suppose he was."

"We never heard of him before. You kept him pretty dark. How did you not bring him home with all the others?"

"Oh. I don't know. He always had to go home and help his mother with the peats or something."

"Mhm? And he's dead you say? How do you know it's him?"

"Well I don't really but the age and the place fits. He worked in East Kilbride."

"There could be dozens of George Campbells in that area. No sense in getting all worked up about it. Drink your tea. It's time you were off to school, isn't it?"

Just like a child again – reduced to size, she thought.

"I suppose so," she said.

And did as she was told.

THE exams were finished. The finals were over. He was pretty gloomy about his hope of anything but a third. She knew she had not done half enough work to warrant a pass in her post-grad diploma but she hardly cared. She felt guiltily that she had distracted him and spoiled his chances.

It was time to go home but graduation from teaching college kept her in Edinburgh while George had to hurry north to work the croft for his widowed mother.

It was their last evening together. The Mallaig train left at 3am, so there was no point in going to bed. The rest of the flat was asleep but they sat on the floor by the light of the electric fire cuddling, stroking, murmuring, trying to ignore the clock.

"Can't you stay just one more day? What will I do without you?"

"Big cat, I can't. I promised to take my little cousin home safely."

"Where is he?"

"He's at Leith Nautical College. He'll be meeting me at Waverley about half-past two."

"Bother him!" She grudged anyone who had claims other than her own.

I'm getting as bad as Duncan, she thought. *I'd better watch out.*

"I'll come to the station with you," she said suddenly. "Please say yes. Every moment is precious."

"All right. I'd like you to come."

It was very warm.

The fire highlighted everything in vermilion. The shadows were hot and black.

"I'm too hot," said George suddenly.

"Take off your shirt then."

"No. I'm shy."

"Don't be daft! There's only me. If you want to be comfortable why not?"

"It's not fair if I do and you don't."

"Eh?" She stared at him, frowning, but he was quite serious.

"Do you mean that?"

"Yes. You take your shirt off and so will I."

"Well, I don't know. I've never had such a bare-faced proposition before."

"Bare-faced?"

They collapsed, giggling, and then captivated by the novelty of his thinking, she stripped off her blouse. The firelight crimsoned her face and shoulders. Laughing, she undid his shirt and hauled it over his head.

"Now we are equal," she said.

"Not quite."

"Well, you are a hard man, George Campbell! All these weeks and now you pounce."

He kissed her gently and they ran their hands over each other and when he undid her bra she made no demur. He was the most seductive man! There was no resistance left in her but once again he bided his time.

It was enough. They had gone a step further in their intimacy. Now this must be savoured and pleasured to the full.

And then it was 2am, cold, dark and real. They had to emerge from their cosy womb. They had to put on their shirts and coats and go shivering into the night.

Waverley was a tomb – grim, brilliant, clanging and deserted. Ticket bought, they sat on an empty bench and presently the cousin from Leith squeezed in beside them.

There was nothing to say. They held hands and stared into space.

Marnie had never felt like this before. There was a hollow gnawing feeling in her belly. How could emptiness have weight? She wanted to hijack him, kidnap him, shang-hai him away from this Wee Free mother who had the prior claim.

The train came. In a trance she saw them board, waved them good-bye, and watched them go out over the clanging points. Then, huddled against the empty world, Marnie went home alone to bed.

His letters filled the void. They came once a week. Back home with her family, she used to sit on the big Caithness flagstone at the door to watch the turn of the road for the postie on his bike. It seemed strange that George's letters should arrive from the east when her whole being was orientated to the west where he was, like a compass needle to its pole.

She kept his letters secret, mentioned them to no one, not even her sister.

It was not that she was ashamed of loving him. She just did not want their relationship mauled by prying questions.

"WHO was this George Campbell anyway? What did he do?" her mother asked.

"Oh, he was just a bloke I knew for a while. He was doing Geography."

"Was he a teacher?"

"No. I don't know what he did in the end. Industry of some sort, I think. I don't know."

"Where was he from?" This one from her father who up until now had been engrossed in his porridge. She groaned. Here it came!

"From Lewis."

"A Leòdhasach! Could you not have done better than that?"

Anger boiled up in her. That remark was so predictable. Her father came from Harris and the rivalry between the two parts of the Long Island was too stupid to bother about now. Silly to get het up about it, yet she was angry. She did not want to discuss it.

"It doesn't matter where he came from. He's dead," she snapped. "Eat your egg, for goodness sake, Davy, and stop wasting it. Do you think eggs grow on trees?"

"No, Mam. They come out of hens' bottoms."

Damn! She couldn't even indulge in a bit of grief without the family turning her tragedy into farce.

While they were all still laughing she shouldered her bag.

"Right I'm off. See you all at lunchtime."

THEY met one lunch-time in a tiny pub at the back of the Old Quad – one they had never been in before. It was crammed over-full with tables and chairs and nobody sat in them at all.

A bored barman leaned on the counter gazing at the oppression of red formica.

Giggling a little at the strangeness of the packed empty room, they took their glasses of stout and squeezed into a corner.

Marnie leaned forward, elbows on the table, to whisper and abruptly the world turned upside-down. The tabletop flipped like a tiddley-wink, firing glasses right over her head, showering the room with stout. For one shocked moment they stared at each other's eyes, at the ruined table and the shattered glasses and then uncontrollable laughter turned them into lunatics. They sat in the wreckage and wept with laughter till the disgusted barman threw them out.

THERE was a postcard from Roddie at lunchtime. "Visited Kate at Thornhill. Going on to Stranraer. Home on Wednesday."

Good. She was missing him. It was time he came home. They had needed this breathing-space but now it was time to go on again.

As marriages went, she supposed theirs was a pretty good one. It was funny to think that, dwelling as she had been on the past, but it was as well to recognise it. It would be all right to have Roddie home again.

WHEN the break came with George it happened bewilderingly quickly.

After the long holidays, George and Marnie greeted each other ecstatically but as the weeks passed they saw each other less often. Marnie was now teaching and finding out how exhausting that could be. Most evenings she dragged herself back to the flat to fall asleep on the sofa. George was away job-hunting without much success. They met when they could.

The flat was less home-like now too. Her closest friend had gone back to Galloway to teach and find herself a young farmer and a new girl had joined them. Marnie felt a bit strange and lonely.

One Sunday afternoon Kate's ex-boyfriend came round. Dan Wilson had been a frequent visitor while Kate had been there but now he was lonely too, abandoned, a relic of Kate's student days. He did not belong to Kate's farming background so he had been left behind. Marnie felt sorry for him. They all liked him and welcomed him back to the flat and the fireside.

At last, tiring of the cramped stuffy room, Marnie tossed aside *The Observer* and stood up.

"I'm away out for a walk. I need to stretch my legs. Anyone coming with me?"

She did not care whether they came or not. She felt empty, restless, melancholy with that sadness peculiar to Sundays. It would be quite nice to be alone but she felt it polite to ask.

Dan Wilson said he would come. None of the others moved, so off they went, matching their strides to each other. It turned into a very long walk – Trinity, Granton, Silverknowes, along the shore to Cramond. By the time they reached there they had achieved an easy sort of intimacy.

The sun was sinking now. Wonderful fairylands of cumulus were making a glamour in the west and the rocks of the foreshore were gleaming black and silver. Boats swung on the ebb tide or lay keeled on the mud banks and the gulls reminded her of home. It was pure cinemascope.

Dan looked a bit like a film star too – tall, handsome – give him a scarf and a gold earring and he could pass for a pirate or a gipsy on any Hollywood set.

When he kissed her it seemed the only thing to do under the circumstances and like an actress in glorious technicolor, she let him. In fact she kissed him back although all the while she was aware only of the romantic picture they must be making.

They could use us for an advertisement, she thought. None of it was real.

They ran for a bus and collapsed panting on the back seat upstairs. He put his arm round her possessively and, having let him kiss her, she did not like to tell him to take it away.

The longer she left it the more the damage was done. By the time the bus reached her stop he seemed to think he had captured her, that she was his. She went home troubled.

Next day she sought out George Campbell and found him in one of their old haunts in the University Common Room. A graduate teacher now, she felt a stranger there.

Guilt and remorse came over her and sadness. Everything was tarnished. Everything had changed.

He was sitting dejectedly toying with his coffee spoon. She had to tell him before someone else did.

"George," she said, "I have something to tell you. When you were away I went for a walk with Dan Wilson. We went to Cramond and I let him kiss me."

He just looked at her and then he said, "Well, I knew it was too good to last. I knew the end had to come soon. I hope you'll be very happy with him." And he got up and walked away.

Stupefied, she gazed at the swinging door. It couldn't be true. She had intended to apologise, to ask forgiveness for a silly aberration. She had not expected him to be overjoyed at her lapse but she had not expected to be cut off with such finality. He was finished with her. No second chances. She had spoiled everything. The door slowly closing told her that. What a fool she had been!

WHY did I not run after him? Why did I not ask for another chance? thought Marnie washing up the lunch dishes.

Why did we let stupid pride form a barrier between us? Who knows? We were very young and I was very silly.

SHE could not take in what had happened and drifted around like a sleepwalker for weeks. Everybody seemed to take it for granted that she had swapped George Campbell for Dan and, dazed as she was, she lacked the energy to contradict them. People even congratulated her. With his looks and his money, Dan was quite a catch. George disappeared from their circle altogether. She heard he had gone to Glasgow.

So she let Dan acquire her. There seemed to be no reason not to. He was pleasant company. He said he had fancied her for a long time. Quite soon they were engaged to be married. She gave up her virginity at last. There seemed to be no reason to hang on to it any longer but for her there was no pleasure in their love-making. It was purely mechanical. Dan was an engineer. He liked machinery.

Life drifted on in a deadly way. On the face of it they made a fine couple.

They bought a house and spent a lot of time examining furniture in shop windows but somehow the final decision about what to buy was always his. His money bought it, so fair enough, she would think to herself and shrug. None of it mattered very much.

A whole year went by. They went home to her parents who welcomed him and approved of him but once she saw him in her own landscape doubts began to nag at her. Life was returning to her frozen mind. She thought of Kate who had left him behind. Now Kate's ruthlessness seemed like kind common-sense.

Small things jarred. She realised that they did not care for the same things at all. It dawned on her that for a year she had subjugated all her interests to his view of things and their value – to property, houses, cars, antiques. He disregarded or laughed at her wish to go to the theatre, see pictures, enjoy the countryside. Their first walk was the only one they ever took. They went everywhere to the roar of vintage engines and eye-watering winds.

Desperation was growing in her. The wedding was to be in April. The hotel was booked. She was sure now she could not go through with it, yet she had no idea how to break off the engagement. She knew fine that her soft-heartedness often led her into committing worse acts of vandalism on people's feelings. Look what she had done to George Campbell.

She was still in a dilemma when the time came to take her class to school camp. Dan was irritated at her going. It smacked too much of independence, but Marnie was delighted at her chance to be herself again.

There was an artist at the camp in charge of entertainments, a small hairy man who leaped about with irrepressible vivacity. She was power-fully attracted to his energy. Roddie gave her a reason for breaking off the engagement. His interests matched her own. He saw the country-side through an artist's eye and machines as tools for living not gods to be worshipped.

Dan was furious. Long, bitter, messy scenes followed until she finally convinced him that she really did not want him. He regarded her interlude at school camp with Roddie as a quite legitimate piece of amusement and admitted airily that he had had quite a few bits on the side himself during the past year or so. That cheered her up. It freed her from any guilt on his behalf.

Once at a party in Glasgow her sister Ellen came upon George Campbell sitting alone on a sofa. They spent the evening together.

"You're *so* like her, he kept saying. "You're *so* like her."

Ellen thought he was lovely but would not let him take her home because it was not herself he was with in spirit but Marnie.

"MAM, when is Dad coming home?"

"Tomorrow, love."

"Will he bring me anything?"

"Maybe. What are you hoping for?"

"A real baseball and a Snoopy book."

"Well, I don't know what he'll bring but it will be good to have him back, won't it?"

"Yes. What's for tea?"

She grieved secretly for George Campbell all week. Then on Friday one of the teachers left a *Press and Journal* on the staff-room table. It caught her eye:

OBAN MAN IN CRASH

George Campbell (36), Dunollie Rd, was killed on Monday night when the car he was driving collided with a lamp-post in East Kilbride. He suffered severe head head injuries amd died at the scene. Campbell, a noted shinty-player, leaves a wife and young family.

In Lewis the men play football. Her George Campbell had never played shinty in his life!

YEARS passed. The boys grew up and went to college. Roddie left for good. Domesticity was stifling him, he said, so he did a Gauguin and left to become a full-time artist.

Alone for the first time in her life, Marnie had time to take stock, re-adjust and look back at the past. She and her sister and a bottle of wine grew confidential one night and the talk went back to George Campbell.

Ellen urged Marnie to find out what had happened to him and Marnie confessed that she had often wished she could but had never had the courage. Indeed she had been to Lewis five years before, visiting friends, and had driven through George's village but had not had the nerve to stop. Instead she had gone to Aignish and wandered above the beach making up poetry as she went, enjoying an agreeable melancholy as she tramped through the wet grass.

"Well, I'm going to Lewis soon. Perhaps I'll have more guts," said Ellen. "Would you mind? After all, I met him too."

"No. I'd like to know how he is."

Marnie forgot about this but her sister did not. She and her husband went to Lewis and when she came back she had a story to tell.

She had gone to the village and knocked on a door, asked some questions and been sent down the road to a Campbell cousin.

Five years before, George, who had never married, was walking home one night from Stornoway when a hit-and-run driver caught him and flung him in the ditch.

He was buried in Aignish.

Ellen offered to go back to Lewis with Marnie but Marnie said no.

She had already been there, whether too early or too late she would never know but it was all the same now. She had suffered the loss and done the grieving and all that was needed was the epitaph —

> *So you were there*
> *five years ago*
> *in Aignish*
> *when I walked alone*
> *through the wet grass*
> *outside the rylock fence;*

There in a numbered plot,
flowers fading
on the wounded turf.
I never knew.
I walked along the machair
writing poetry
enjoying melancholy
for no good reason
and all the while,
mo rùn geal òg,
you lay so close beside me
in the black ground.

Bonnie George Campbell.

OVER THE SEA TO . . . ?

IT IS strange to drive down to a ferry in the middle of a long journey, to find after ravelling back the miles hour upon hour that suddenly there is no more road. You have to stop and you have to wait, for the road has slid under the water and you are at the mercy of the ferryman.

Mary had been roaring down the road as fast as wind and weather would allow, hurtling through chasms of darkness into a vortex of rain and sleet. Her wheels slashed across great pools, sending up a bow-wave as high as the car.

After the lonely dark it was almost cosy on the slipway. The big arc lights seemed to keep the night and weather at bay and the brightly lit ferry was sitting at the water's edge like a squat scallop.

Two other cars were already on board and just under the bridge was a small blue furniture van.

There was nobody on the rain-lashed deck to guide her so she drove straight on and parked near the life raft, taking a lane to herself. Easy for a quick getaway. Nobody would bother on a night like this about neat parking.

Almost as soon as she had switched off the ignition the boat's engines began to rev. The shudder as the boat took to the sea transmitted through deck plates and car wheels to Mary.

"Good! We're off," she thought. "No time lost at all." A quick cross-ing and an hour's drive and she would be getting a homely welcome in Lochcarron. It was a happy prospect on such a miserable night.

She glanced idly through the blurred windscreen. Not a soul had appeared on deck. It was stormier than she had realised. She began to wish she had stayed at home. The boat, for all its squat strength, was heaving and plunging, smacking down on the waves so that spume spouted up between the ramp and the deck. Spindrift gusted along the wavecrests.

Mary wiped her windscreen clear for a few minutes to watch the blue metal sides of the van rippling in the wind until a violent flurry of sleet obliterated the view. Before she could switch on the wipers again a squall struck. The gale boomed and thundered.

The lights of the boat abruptly went out and the engine note struggled. The boat shuddered and heaved, wallowing as a great weight of water broke over it broadside. Mary felt the car slew round under her.

Time hung in the balance, poised on an eternity of terror and disbelief; terror in a welter of water and roaring dark.

Then the lights came on again. The engine sound returned to normal and the boat throbbed on.

Mary discovered that panic had brought her out of the car on to the streaming deck. The wind was tearing her feet from under her. She clung to the ropes of the liferaft, drenched, teeth chattering. Idiot! She bolted back to the car and wrapped a rug round her shoulders.

Just then a figure in oilskins came out of the passenger cabin, a deep hood covering his face. Leaning on the wind, he began to make a round of the cars, collecting fares as if nothing had happened.

Mary reached for her bag and felt in the pockets for her book of season tickets. She picked the yellow stubs out of a muddle of paper hankies, credit cards and till receipts and held them between her teeth while she stuffed the rubbish back. She was still shivering.

The ferryman loomed outside the window. As she wound it down he surprised her by leaning in and taking the tickets from her mouth. This oddly intimate gesture gave her a queer sensation in the pit of her stomach.

She peered at him crossly to see if it was anybody she knew taking liberties but the cowl of his hood over the peaked cap obscured his face completely. His hands were blotched and toadlike.

"What a terrible squall that was!" she said. "I thought we had had it."

He did not reply but stared at her tickets.

"What's the matter? They're not out of date are they?"

"It's usually coins," he said.

"Coins yourself! It's pound notes on this ferry and soon it will be fivers! It costs a king's ransom nowadays. That's why I got the book of tickets. They're much cheaper."

"Coins are better," he mumbled, rattling his leather pouch. Abruptly he handed her book back and scudded crabwise into the shelter of the cabin.

"Miserable old so and so!" Mary thought. "He probably fiddles the takings."

The boat churned on through the dark. It seemed to get blacker by the minute. Surely it was time to see some lights on the other side even on a night like this. Mary peered forward but nothing could be seen. She risked getting out for a moment and stole a look over the side of the ferry; nothing there either but the howl of the black wind and the pitching, tossing sea. Unease began to turn to dread. There ought to be lights on the far shore.

She had a desperate urge to speak to someone, to share her misgivings. With the rug over her head like a shawl, she fought her way across the deck to the blue van and banged on the door. The wind nearly whipped it out of her hand.

"Hey! Mind ma door, hen," yelled a cheery youth over a blast of rock music from the tape-deck.

"Hurry up and come on in. You're letting in a helluva draught."

"I came to see if you'd noticed," Mary bawled. "Something's wrong. We should be across by now. We must be off course. I can't see any lights. I don't know where we are."

"Och! It's like that a' the time, hen. Here. Stop panicking and have a sandwich. It's meat paste and cheese. What's your hurry anyway?"

"It's not the hurry. It's just – well – everything's gone all queer. Something's wrong and I'm scared. You're not from here, are you?"

"Naw. I just cam up frae Leith wi' a load o' stuff for Portree and I'm on my way back. I've never been in this part o' the world before an' ye can keep it. It's no a patch on Leith Walk. See thae pubs!"

"Listen. I've been over this ferry hundreds of times. We should be there by now. It doesn't take that long to cross and we should be able to see the lights on both slipways all the time. We must be heading out to sea. I'm going to see if anyone else knows what's happened."

"Aye. Away ye go, hen, but I'm telling you – it'll be OK and if it's no – well there's bugger a' we can dae aboot it."

Once again Mary struggled into the foul night. Sleet lashed her legs and she had to stagger backwards against the wind to be able to breathe at all.

The windows of the nearest car were all steamed up and the driver was very reluctant to open it when she knocked on the glass. He had a tight disapproving face.

"What is it? What do you want?"

"Excuse me but haven't you noticed how long the boat's taking to make the crossing. We should have been there by now."

"What's she saying, Duncan?" His wife leaned over suspiciously. He ignored her.

"Yes we have noticed. We're locals – from Glen Shiel. I think the captain is going up the coast so that he can shelter. The current is probably too strong to let us cross at the ferry tonight."

"We could be away up the loch then. What'll we do?" wailed Mary.

"Do? What can we do? The captain knows best. Put your trust in him."

"But why can't we see any lights? It's all horrible without any lights. That's why I'm frightened."

"There's probably been a power cut. Now go and get under shelter, girl. You're soaked."

He wound up the window.

Mary stared at the streaked glass for a moment then turned and dived for the passenger cabin. Even the dour ferryman would be better company then being shut alone in her own wee box.

But when she wiped the rain from her eyes there was no sign of the ferryman.

The long metal passageway was empty except for a dark-haired man in a donkey-jacket and orange PVC trousers. He was taking a swig out of a quarter-bottle and when he saw her bedraggled state he grinned and held out the bottle.

"Do you fancy a dram? You look as if you could do with one."

"Oh yes please! Slàinte!" She tilted the bottle and the whisky exploded gloriously in her stomach. Strength returned to her knees.

"Thank you very much. I really needed that."

She sat down beside him on the long slatted bench.

"Did you see the ferryman? I thought he came in here. What's happening? Why are we taking so long?"

"Och here! One question at a time! There was nobody around when I came in. I came to look for him myself and I haven't a clue what's happening. Something pretty queer by the looks of things."

"I'm scared. I tried to talk to the other folk out there but one lot seems to think they'll be OK if they sit tight and trust the captain and the other guy doesn't give a hoot."

"Well. I've been back and fore on this ferry many's a time and it has never been like this before. Maybe if there has been a massive blackout the skipper has lost his landmarks and gone off course. Look. You're shivering. Come over here a bit and I'll keep you warm. Share the rug. Come on! I won't bite you. We might as well make the best of things. My name's Archie, by the way."

He was a nice-looking fellow, Mary decided and his offer seemed kindly meant, so she cuddled into the crook of his arm and accepted another swig of whisky. She felt braver now – comforted.

"Where were you going?" she asked.

"I live over at Erebusaig. My parents have a croft. I usually work at the prawns with my brother but I've been labouring at the new road to get some cash."

"Did the ferryman say anything to you about the blackout?"

"Not a thing. He's away with the fairies, yon one. He wanted the fare in fifty pees. I told him I hadn't drunk that much but he wasn't amused. He was narking on about needing coins so I managed to dig out two. That's all he wanted so I gave up trying to hand him the rest. He'll not last long in the job at that rate!"

The boat ploughed on. Time passed slowly and more slowly.

The pulse of the engines and reaction to shock and cold made Mary and her companion drowsy.

Conversation faltered and died and they dozed, snuggled against one another.

Waves creamed past the metal sides. Occasionally the squat-ramped hull smacked a comber into a fountain of spray but the sea was quieter now. The clouds were higher. They travelled on under a black and starless sky. There seemed to be no future and no past – just a brightly lit boat with its dazed load of passengers in transit, suspended between then and there.

MARY stirred and stretched a cramped muscle. Her bottom ached from the imprints of the slats. Suddenly she sprang awake.

"Look! Look, Archie! Lights. We're there. Oh, thank Goodness! We've arrived. We'll be all right now."

Through the open door the twinkling lights of the ferry terminal reached across the water in shimmering ribbons. The sea had dropped. The wind had died.

"Archie, wake up! We're nearly there. We'd best get back to the cars."

"What? Oh! Right enough. That's great." He scrambled to his feet. "Come on then."

They started forward along the metal gangway and then stopped to look at each other. "Thank you," she said, "For being good to me. I was awfully scared."

"So was I. And lonely too. Thank *you*."

He bent forward and gave her a wee kiss.

"Ships that pass in the night, eh? I hope we meet again."

"Me too, Archie. Take care now."

Mary staggered stiffly back to her car. They were close to the shore now and she expected the ferry to sail into the jetty with its usual lack of delay but something further was wrong. The boat stood off from the quay, engines thrashing. The passengers who had been on the alert in their cars slumped again and began to come out to see what the matter was now.

The ferryman appeared and seemed to study the ramps. A figure on the shore pulled out towards them in a small dinghy.

Curiosity got the better of Mary too. She joined the small group on the deck, wondering and speculating. The ferryman ignored them, his hooded face turned towards the dinghy. They decided among themselves that the storm must have damaged the ramp mechanism. The approaching mechanic would put it right.

While she waited, leaning on the rail, Mary studied the nearby shore. There were the bright lights of the village clustered cheerfully round the slipway and beyond them the dark desolate moorland – myrtle and heather and bog asphodel the only growing things for miles. Over to the left though, the sky was strangely lurid. A red glow reflected back from the low cloud ceiling. What was that? Surely not the Kishorn Yard. The oil platforms were not so near. That red glow looked evil, sombre and threatening.

Mary shivered and looked away in the other direction. To the right there was darkness – utter darkness – outer darkness. Her teeth were chattering with the cold.

"Hell, I wish this infernal voyage was over!" she thought.

She watched the engineer climb aboard and confer with the ferryman. They were in no hurry.

Beyond the slipway was a huge road sign. For lack of anything better to do she screwed up her eyes to read it. Bright lights dazzled off its wet surface. The letters came and went. Familiar placenames seemed somehow wrong. The sign jarred on her nerves.

She overheard Archie and the vanman talking.

"I cam frae Leith."

"Leith, eh?"

"LETHE!"

Something clicked in Mary's head. A white light burst in her brain.

"Stop!" she yelled at them. "Wait! I've just realised. This is not Kyle. This is Hell. They've tricked us. Once we get off the ferry we are dead. Something must have happened to us on the way over. Something in the storm."

They stared at her.

"Listen! It all fits. You're going to Lethe, the river of forgetfulness."

83

She turned on Archie. "And you are going to Erebus over the moor beyond the Asphodel fields."

And *you* – " she pointed to the Strict Presbyterian couple "– you are bound for Sheol, the Hebrews' place of death. Oh! It all fits! And me, I'm headed for Acheron, tributary of the Styx. Hicks for the Styx! That's us!"

And Mary began to laugh, near to tears.

"Hmph!" said the woman from Glen Shiel. "Too much education has turned that one's head. I thought she sounded a bit hysterical. Come on, Duncan, they've sorted the ramps. I'm not staying to listen to any more of that heathenish rubbish."

She dragged at her husband's arm and they climbed into their Ford.

The fellow from Leith grinned at Archie and tapped his forehead.

"She's aff her heid. Shame that! She's no a bad-looking burd. Aye weel, back on the job! Edinburra, here I come!"

The van spluttered and roared over the ramp in a blast of heavy metal.

Mary looked despairingly at Archie.

"Can't you see? That's the way to Hell. All the road signs are different.

"Look hard and you will see not what you expect to see but what is really there.

"Archie, the road should go uphill from the ferry but look! It slopes down. *'Facilis descensus Averno'*. Easy is the descent into Hell.

Oh, *why* can't I make you understand?" She was really crying now.

Archie patted her arm.

"Look love. I'm sorry. I shouldn't have given you all that whisky. It's gone to your head. I think you'd better book in at the hotel for the night. Now, I'm sorry to leave you like this but I really must be going."

He jumped into his car and shot off the ferry down the road to Erebus.

Mary turned on the ferryman.

"I know why they couldn't see what I saw. They all paid you in coins, didn't they? Coins are the proper fare, aren't they, Charon? But you couldn't refuse my season ticket and you have no real power over me. HELL, NO! And what's more – I've prepaid my return ticket. You'll *have* to take me back!"

She ran to the car and flung herself in. The ticket-book was on the passenger seat. She waved it at hooded Charon and switched on the ignition. The car roared. She slammed it into gear and did a spectacular U-turn on the empty deck, turning her back on the infernal road sign and setting her face to the dark waters once more.

The boat slid away from the jetty and all the lights went out.

THE TAIRSGEIR

"SOMEONE has started cutting right next to our peats."
"What! Where?"
"Along the old drain that runs into our bank."
"Did you see them?"
"No. There was nobody there just the cut peats. They've spread across our track to the stile."
"What! Mairi's voice was rising. Her blood was rising too, in a way that surprised her. She felt threatened.

The peatbank, about three miles out of the village, was a place away from the prying, gossiping eyes of the street. It was a sanctuary of space and peace. And now somebody was crowding them close. A robin could not have felt more hostile to the intruder than she did.

"Have they cut much? Have they kept off our spread?"
"Well, they've spread a bit on our side of the ditch, her husband admitted. "You'll see for yourself tomorrow."

They planned to start cutting next day. When they first came to the island from Edinburgh, Mairi had shown Neil how to cut peats. It was part of her heritage; she had absorbed it from watching her father at work.

Neil was a city lad but eager to learn. In those days very few people cut peats. All the locals were installing oil-fired central heating or proudly declaring themselves all-electric. Now, in a recession with money short and fuel prices rising, the hillside was dotted with fresh peat-cuttings again.

Mairi brooded on the intrusion on their small bit of moor.

"The whole wide world to choose from and they have to crowd in on top of us!"

She had lost her peace of mind. She lost it still further the next morning when Neil came back from skinning the bank, a job she could not do because the surface divots were too heavy for her to lift.

"Remember Murdy MacPhee, the tinker boy, who was on that 3C class we both taught? Well, it's him and another of his relations who are cutting next to us."

"Did you speak to them? Did you ask if they had permission from the grazings committee?"

"Well, no. What right had I to object? They've as much right to cut peats as we have."

"Away you go! You're far too soft. You'd let anyone walk all over you."

"I suppose I am. I just have this thing about other people's liberties."

"At the expense of *our* liberties! Don't be daft!"

Mairi could hardly wait until Neil had taken his soup. She was spoiling for a fight. The violence of her feelings astonished her. She remembered words spoken late one night long ago when they were courting.

"I'm basically a pacifist," she had told Neil. "But I will fight like a wildcat if anyone threatens my territory."

They drove out to the moor and unloaded the car thermos flask and biscuits, midge cream, boots, a spade and the old tairsgeir, given to them by Hecky the Post, who had no more need of it. Every year he asked how it was. Its blade was honed away to a thin slip of iron; its wood had the patina of antiquity, steeped in bog acid, smoothed by years of labouring hands. Mairi loved using the tairsgeir; Neil preferred a spade.

From the road she could see the tinkers. They had moved to a second bank at a slight distance. That one belonged to their uncle and obviously they were cutting for the whole family. A fine wall of peats stood at the edge of the new bank. It was ruler straight and spaced like a soft brick wall with gaps for the wind to whistle through. Even in her irritation Mairi could not help admiring their craft.

To get to the bank she had to stand on some of the newly cut peats. It went against the grain to do this. She resented having to spoil good peats; she resented her loss of freedom. Their beaten path of fifteen years had been quite obvious through the heather and flattened moss.

Mairi's first arrival at the moor had always been a precious moment. The long strip of naked peat waited to be pared off in turves, which were spread out on the heather to harden, then turned and stood on end in little wigwams of three and four to dry out completely before the harvest-home to the stack or the shed. There was the prospect of hours of hard work in the fresh air, the good exercise, the tranquillity and freedom of the moor and at last the reward of security and warmth in the winter to come.

Here and now at the top of the bank was nothing but aggravation. Neil had understated the situation. Not only was their access impeded but a large mass of cut peat covered the moor where the Murchisons needed to spread their crop. Empty bread-wrappers blew in the wind.

Mairi bounded over the heather to where the two MacPhees were bending and cutting, lifting and throwing rhythmically. Two small men, bonnets pulled low over their noses, tattered dungarees and wellingtons, she towered over them, an Amazon in climbing boots.

"Did you get permission to cut that bank? "

Her voice would have done the cutting for them. They knew trouble when they saw it and adopted defensive attitudes. They ignored her question.

"You are cutting far too close to our bank. You've blocked our path to the stile and you have spread your peats across our spread. We've been cutting peats here for fifteen years and never a bit of bother have we had until now."

The older man blustered a little. "We're not blocking your path at all."

"Oh yes you are. Come and see. And *have* you got permission?"

"Yes. Cally said we could cut that old bank." The young MacPhee obviously remembered his days in the classroom. He answered her meekly.

They strode across the bog to the Murchisons' bank and studied the problem.

"You see. That's our path covered with your peats and we need to spread all the way back up there where your peats are now. That cutting was never meant as a peat bank. It's a drainage ditch but if you had kept to the other side of the ditch and left us room to go through there would have been no problem."

The older man capitulated suddenly.

"Come on, Murdy. We'll shift them," he sighed.

"Good! Thank you.

She turned her back on them to hide her relief and gazed across the small river to the ridge of hills. Neil, who had stood apart all this time, a man in the middle distance, unfroze and began to dig. The MacPhees trudged to and fro, moving peats further and further away.

She felt sorry for them and their additional labour, quite sympathetic now she had won the day, but made no offer of help. It was their affair.

Urgent to begin working herself, she took up the peat-iron and made the first slanting incision on the outer face of the bank.

Gradually the sods piled up, a tumble of glistening slabs. Mairi began to lay them out in neat rows below the cut bank. They did not dry so well there but she did not feel like waiting for the tinkers to finish. She had to be doing something.

The MacPhees worked quietly and steadily, murmuring to each other in their own particular Gaelic. Eventually they had cleared a reasonable area, then meekly they enquired, "Will that be enough, do you think?"

Mollified, she nodded.

"Yes. I think we'll manage with that but you'll need to clear the path as well. We can't get past."

They obeyed, tossing the peats further out on the heather and replacing the Murchison's plank of driftwood across the narrow ditch.

"It's not a very good batten, this!" Said one.

"Damned cheek!" Thought Mairi. "They're getting cocky again."

"You shouldn't have put your first cut down on the bottom of the bank," Murdy advised her.

This was too much.

"I know that!" she snapped. "I'd have put them on the high bank if you'd left me a place to put them."

They said no more until the track was cleared.

"Will that do now?"

"Yes. that'll be fine, thanks."

And, "Thanks," Neil echoed from the far end of the peat-bank.

The work progressed peacefully. Cut and lift, cut and lift, cut and lift and throw.

Neil could carry a few peats at a time on his spade. Mairi threw hers into a plastic ball-barrow and trundled it across the wiry tussocks to lay out the neat herringbones of peat, gradually covering heather and lichen and moss. The MacPhees worked in the old style, one cutting, and the other with bent back down in the bog, catching and lifting and throwing the peats out onto the moor. Hard work that – woman's work as a rule but Mairi and Neil had long since found they got on better working to their own rhythm.

Cutting peats alone is backbreaking, boring and repetitive. It leaves the mind free to wander. Normally Mairi switched off and listened to the small sounds of the moor, the burn, the cark of a raven on the crags, the ecstasy of the skylarks. Now and then a passing local would break the monotony with a toot and a wave, acknowledging their return to the peats. Sometimes tourists stopped to snatch a quick photograph of the aborigines before scuttling back to their cars. The Murchisons watched them covertly, amused as always.

"The MacPhees make far better local colour than we do."

"Yes. They look right in the landscape. They blend. We may have been here first but they are indigenous."

Over the heather all afternoon came the smell of fag-smoke and the noise from the tinkers' transistor, the frenetic gabble of a football commentator coming and going on the breeze. When the football was finished they switched to a cassette. Hebridean Hawaii treacled across the moor. The skylarks gave up in disgust.

"What has happened to me?" Mairi wondered. "I am not as irritated by that sort of pollution as I usually am. Neil's live-and-let live philosophy must be getting to me." In actual fact, the MacPhees in her landscape were opening up fresh lively channels of thought and she was enjoying herself.

Neil and Mairi took their thermos of coffee down to the bank of the burn and lay awhile basking in the sun.

"My back's getting a bit sore. Is yours?"

"Yes. I'm stiff. It's all the bending that does it. Never mind. We'll have a day off tomorrow. Can't cut peats on the Sabbath."

"It's funny, that. I thought I'd got rid of most of these taboos from my childhood but that's one I cannot break. I don't even want to. Yet I bought some bedding plants to put in the garden tomorrow. Why can I break the Sabbath planting flowers and not cut peats?"

"Because it's one of the last vestiges of the old traditional way of life, that's why."

"I suppose so. And gardening isn't?"

A caterpillar looped lost along her trouser-leg and she helped it on to a sprig of myrtle.

When they returned to their bog, the Macphees were watching and began to walk purposefully towards them.

"Now what?" Mairi wondered, feeling no trouble in the air.

"Is everything all right now?" They asked in soft voices. "Have you enough room?"

It was a peace mission and it was received amicably.

"Yes. I think we'll manage."

"We wouldn't have got our peats mixed up anyway. They're a different pattern to yours."

Mairi surveyed her peats ruefully. Pattern was hardly the word. No two were the same.

"Right enough. Ours are all shapes and sizes. How do you get yours so perfect?" (Admitting your own inadequacies takes away the power of your opponent's critical thought.)

"Och,it's just the different shape of our peat-iron. Mine has a wider shaft and a shorter blade. Let me see yours a minute."

Mairi handed up the tairsgeir and the tinker looked at it briefly then gave it back.

"You're sure you have plenty of room?"

They hadn't but concessions had to be made.

"Yes. It should be all right."

The overture was at an end. The men returned to their work.

Two seconds later, the head fell off the tairsgeir.

Mairi gazed at it in utter astonishment. So firmly had the iron shoe and the aged smoothed wood been melded together they had seemed all of a piece. It had never even wobbled, yet now, at her very first cut, the head had slid off the shaft like butter off a hot knife.

"Neil! Neil!" she hissed. "Come here a minute."

"What is it?" He called from the end of the bank.

"Sssh!"

"Why are you whispering?"

"Sssh! Keep your voice down. The head has come off the tairsgeir."

Neil came and examined it. Mairi stood close beside him, making herself as large as possible. She did not want the tinkers to see the broken tairsgeir and gloat. She could not believe the feelings that were coming over her.

"Do you think they put the buisneach on the tairsgeir?"

"The evil eye? Is that what you think?" Neil looked at her in astonishment. He seemed to have been doing nothing else all day.

"Well, it's very weird, isn't it, that as soon as he touched it, it fell apart."

"You don't believe that, do you?"

"I don't know. I just don't know."

"He didn't wrench it, did he?"

"No. You saw him yourself. He took it from me across the flat of his two hands and then he sort of stroked the blade very lightly. He didn't force it in any way."

"Well it's no use now. You'd better go home and get a bit of stick to wedge the head back on again. There's nothing you can do here."

Mairi scuttled across the moor, the two pieces of the broken tairsgeir clutched to her chest. She threw them into the car and sped off home, conviction growing in her that the MacPhees had done the mischief to get back at her. But the educated part of her mind stood aghast at such deep-rooted primitive superstition.

She thought hard as she drove down to Ronavaig. She had to accept that they were all one. The ancient and modern co-existed in her just as in the tinkers.

They polluted the environment with noise and litter but they had far more innate knowledge of living with the land than she had. She had a university education and a city husband but her acquired sophistication had no power against her deep awareness of more primitive forces.

She laughed suddenly. There was a strange power in her that afternoon and she was enjoying it. She visualised the sliver of wood she would need to wedge the head back on to the tairsgeir and when she arrived home there it was beside the chopping-block. In a few minutes she had jammed it into place and was back in business.

Nobody acknowledged her return and neither did she. They worked on steadily until the bank was cut and then they went home.

But that was not quite the end of it. Mairi now had a story to tell and as it formed in her mind and shaped with the telling she found there were people who would listen and accept it and others who would rubbish it right away. These people were never Highlanders. It was a great comfort to her to find that her own blood relations, however religious, would be ahead of her with cries of, *"The Buisneach!"* as soon as she described the head falling off the tairsgeir.

The peats dried in the summer wind and were carried home. Next year, when the Murchisons went to cut their bank there was no sign of the MacPhees. No sign at all, except that the peats on the disputed piece of moor had never been lifted, never been touched. They were sinking into the heather now, saturated by a winter's frost and rain. Once again they were in Mairi's way and this time she had to shift them herself to make room.

And the next season they were still there, rotten now and useless. Mairi thought about the buisneach again. Had the MacPhees sensed the strange power she had had that day? Had they abandoned these peats because they felt she had put the eye on *them*? Of course, that was all nonsense. Wasn't it? But if she and her family could believe with even a tiny bit of their minds that the tinkers had the power to damage the tairsgeir by the power of their minds, why should the MacPhees not believe that she had similar powers?

She had no feeling whatever that the peats had been left as a peace offering and it was with a great sense of relief that she lifted them all and threw them back into the bog.

The moor was clean again.

PEATSMOKE

Peat smoke is blue
And rich with memories,
The scent of heather, grass and moss,
Dead leaves and turf
And falaisgean in spring,
The summer sun
And winter rains,
Backache, exhaustion,
Midge-bites stinging in your sweat,
Laughter and tea
out on the open moor.
The company of family and friends,
The tairsgeir, the spade
And brown-stained hands
Clotted with chocolate mud.
Wild thyme and heather-bells
And dancing cotton-grass.
A skylark singing
Hanging in the air.
A raven carking on the crags
And cuckoos in the birchwood
By the burn.

Peat smoke is whisky
Golden in the glass,
A ceilidh by a friendly hearth
Safe from the lashing rain
With talk and music
Round the dancing flames
The wind outside
Mourning its loneliness
Around the chimney-pots
And sometimes blowing back the smoke
With fragrant spite.
Red embers in the morning
Under the soft grey ash,
A fireside blessing
Ancient as the moor
Remembered while you clean the hearth
And pile the rough brown blocks
Of captured sunlight
Round the glow
To warm another day.

THE BROCH

THE broch clung to the hillside like a barnacle. Inside its stone ring there was peace and a sense of security.

"All the people who ever came here have left their feelings behind," thought Meg. "It's like a big stone hug."

She imagined mothers crouching in the galleries, holding their children close while their men guarded the entrances and the thwarted enemy prowled outside.

What did they fear then? Death was a fact of life. Slavery more likely. To be parted from their own kind; to be alienated and used that would be the worst thing. But life was always precious and the instinct for survival must have led these seemingly simple farmers and drovers to build their fortresses, their hollow hills, perfect machines for defence.

The July sun beat on her shoulder blades. The air above the stones was shimmering. Meg leaned against the breastwork of the outer wall and gazed down the glen, dreaming.

Below the broch was a neat farm, trim whitewashed buildings set among green fields. When she had climbed up to the broch the home park behind the house had been full of quiet, watchful sheep, newly clipped. Their eyes had followed her all the way up the hill. Now they exploded into confusion. The farmer and his son had come from the house and were herding the ewes and lambs into the maze of the fank to separate the hoggets from their mothers. It was time to put these adolescent sheep out on their own. Their sheltered time was over; now they must fend for themselves.

Meg looked down on the pattern of movement with pleasure. The creamy-backed sheep poured like liquid through the tubes of the fank, now pouring this way, now surging back, stamping and skittering about in bewilderment, churning the grass to mud.

The stones of the fank were the stones of the broch but divisive, separated, put to an opposite use.

Men stood at the narrow gate turning aside the ewes, ejecting the little curly hoggets between the nettles and the foxgloves. They leaped and bleated with pleasure at their freedom, jumped the burn and then stood facing the walls, irresolute, not knowing where to turn without their mothers.

The bleating became more pitiful with each new bereavement; deep-throated mourning from the ewes in the fold, little pitiful calls from the wee sheep outside. It tore at Meg's heart and caught her by the throat. It was all in the order of things she knew. The men at the gate could not afford to be sentimental. The parting had to come some day, be it animal or human but Meg knew how the sheep felt; it had happened to her once too.

SHE was standing at the big front door of the castle watching her parents climb into their car. They were about to leave her to begin her secondary education at the Academy. She felt sick with misery and excitement and terror. The prospect of secondary school was frightening enough after her tiny village school, but to be left to face it on one's own, to have to live in a hostel of seventy girls, strangers, in this big castle was more than she could bear. She wanted to cry out, "Stop! Don't leave me. Take me away." But instead Meg stood there, self-contained, too proud to let her feelings show, a forlorn little figure in pigtails and white ankle socks, trying to smile.

At all costs the parents must not know how bad she was feeling. They might be upset. It was all right for them though. They had each other and her sister and they were going back to the beloved country, going home. The thought of all she was parted from tore at her. She stared hard, mouth set.

"I will not cry. I must not cry. Nobody will know how I am feeling. Nobody."

Her father had turned the car now on the gravel drive. They waved from the windows.

"Goodbye. Be a good girl. Write soon. Goodbye."

And they were away. Her heart welled up in her throat. Everything she had was deserting her. She had no idea what lay ahead. She was utterly on her own.

For ages, she stood staring at the empty air where the car had been, as if she could conjure it back. Her whole being was concentrated into a tiny spot deep inside her, shut away and battened down against the hostile world.

Stiff and cold and hard, she turned to go inside. The huge door was very heavy. It took all her strength to shut it behind her.

"I was like the broch," thought Meg, running her hand over the glittering grey stone. "I built myself a hard round shell so that my vulnerability was safe from attack. It was all I could do. It worked too. I was considered a very cool customer. Nobody knew how insecure I was inside."

She looked down at the lonely little sheep, bereft and bleating dismally.

"I'm glad my sons don't have to leave home when they are twelve. It's far too young."

It suddenly struck her that she had never until that moment appreciated what her mother must have suffered at having to give her up. In a flash, the ewes' distress made her realise that her parents had undoubtedly missed her too.

Her mind took another jump to the recent High School prize-giving, which she had attended both as parent and member of staff.

THE hall was full – pupils, parents, potted plants and prizes, teachers and tartan rugs, and the minister's wife in a desperate hat. The speeches droned on. Everyone sat to attention, minds wandering. The dignitaries put a polish on their platitudes and time went on its holidays.

The headmaster rose to sum up the year with the usual farewells to school-leavers and the customary welcomes and warnings to the innocents about to enter secondary school. This year the clichés had meaning for Meg. Her son was in the front row, wide-eyed and proud. Next term he would be in the big school. Meg was thankful that they had found a place to bring up children where parting would not be necessary.

The headmaster was talking about building now, deploring the over-centralisation of house-building on the island, pointing out that the rural communities were dying and the town was growing too fast. The school hostels were emptying; one had been closed already. Houses, he said, should be built in the villages to keep the rural communities vital to save the small primary schools from closure.

Meg thought he had a point. She taught in the town's primary school and knew the problems of over-crowding they suffered. She clapped enthusiastically. Good! Now for the prizes. Soon they would be free to go. Soon the summer holidays would begin.

THE ewes were still wailing as she left the broch; a cluster of little hoggets still hung round, like adolescents at a chip-shop. Others were drifting away, dejected.

As Meg went down the sunny road she noticed some sheep up on the hill still with their lambs. They had a short spell of togetherness left. Meg thought of the people moving into the town.

"Who can blame them? Are they not doing what we did avoiding the need to put their children into a hostel? We are all of us clinging to ways to avoid separation, from the Picts in their broch to the sheep in the hidden places of the hill. We are all the same."

The noise of the fank was fading into the distance but the lamentation would go on all night. Sheep would wander distractedly trying to find their own until the hurt began to ease and they forgot.

For them next year would bring another lamb.

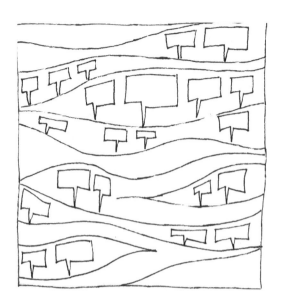

THE SOFT PRESENT

A plane droned over the hospital garden, mohair on blue chiffon. Meg dropped her embroidery and gazed drowsily upwards. Maybe Carlyle was on that plane heading for Manhattan.

She rolled over on the grass. Bees buzzed in the honeysuckle, heavy with summer.

"I'm glad I'm down here," she thought, rich with satisfaction. "I may be shut in for now but I'm freer than he is."

A small wooden notice stuck in the lawn said, "PLEASE KEEP HOT TEAPOTS OFF THE GRASS".

It had bothered her with its surreal message ever since she had come to the hospital; it left her vaguely pondering. Come to think of it, the notice symbolised the homeopathic way, the ethos of this place. It was effective; she had never seen a teapot hot or cold anywhere near the grass.

Yet it was mysterious too.

"How does homeopathy work?" she wondered. "How can a minute dose of something heal more potently than a large one? It can't all be placebo." It made little scientific sense, yet she trusted homeopathy completely now that she had see it produce dramatic results in herself. This extraordinary hospital had helped her find strength and self-confidence, the power to overcome the allergies that had previously crippled her. She had thrown away her crutches and now walked free.

The bees hummed in the sunshine. Pollen hung heavy on the air and Meg drifted off to sleep on the perfect green grass.

VERA sat up in bed, a little shrew of a woman, grey in colour except for the black beady eyes glittering behind her glasses. She was crippled with arthritis.

"Come on, hen, you're aw right as long as you have the use of your legs," she cackled.

Indomitably cheerful, she would hurl herself to and fro on her Zimmer, screeching with laughter and cracking jokes but now and again nurses would find the patients in Vera's vicinity tearful and depressed. Vera had her magic of the minimum dose too. A drop of malice in just the right spot could set a patient festering with resentment or wilting with misery.

Outside the hospital Vera had nobody. Nobody came to visit her. Nobody cared. When her treatment was finished she had nowhere to go; the hospital kept prolonging her treatment.

She was in a sunny mood today. The other patients wanted their fortunes told and this was something Vera did well. It made her the focus of attention for a while. Poor Vera became Power Vera, the truth-teller, the mouth of the oracle.

"Come and get your fortune read, Meg," one of the women called. "Come on. It's a laugh."

"Och, I never bother with that sort of thing. The present is as much as I can cope with." Then, seeing Vera's crestfallen face, she capitulated.

"Oh, all right. Come on then. What do I have to do?"

Vera riffled the cards deftly and cut them with a snap. She fanned them face down.

"Pick fourteen cards from anywhere in the pack but don't go backwards in your picking. Always from right to left." She droned the words solemnly, a priestess at a ritual.

Meg giggled a little. "I don't really believe all this stuff. I've always avoided having my fortune told. This is the first time."

"Give me your chosen cards," intoned Vera. The other patients waited expectantly.

"Now, hen, you understand, I have the gift and I use it to amuse folk. You needn't take it too seriously."

"Yes, yes. There's no ace of spades, is there?" She was nervous in spite of herself.

"No, hen. You've a good hand here. Someone you know is going to have a baby. You'll know of a friend who's expecting, likely."

"No, Vera. I don't think so.

"Well, you'll be hearing soon."

"As long as it's not myself!"

They all laughed.

"There's a fair man in your life who will cross deep water and a dark woman friend who is very fond of you who is going abroad. Aye, she's thinking of you."

None of this made much sense to Meg but she kept trying to think of ways Vera's predictions might come true, just to please her.

"There will be changes at home and good fortune and a tall, dark, ambitious man is very near and coming closer. Aye. He'll bring you a soft present. Do you know anyone like that, hen?"

"Yes, Vera. I do, as a matter of fact."

Thoughts of Carlyle sprang into Meg's mind. It was his ambition that had separated them all those years ago when she thought her heart would break. He had gone away to get on in a world where she could not follow.

"Do you think this tall, dark, ambitious man will come to see you here?"

"I don't know. It's possible but very unlikely. Watch out for him, girls. He's rich. Maybe he'll bring me a mink coat!"

NEXT morning Meg was at her embroidery in the garden when a nurse appeared at the door.

"You have a visitor. It is not the correct time so you will have to see him out here. And not for long, mind! It's nearly lunch-time."

"All right, nurse. Thank you."

Carlyle's large bulk filled the doorway.

"Carlyle! I was thinking about you just yesterday. Do you know – one of the patients saw you coming in the cards."

He ignored her chatter, asked polite questions about her health but scarcely listened to the answers. He wanted only to talk about himself, about the business deal he was going to clinch in New York, about the tycoon he was going to meet, whose face was on the front page of every newspaper that day because of the takeover bid he had spearheaded.

Meg studied him while he droned on. She had loved this man once with a passion that had nearly destroyed her life. She had given him up because of his career and her marriage and breaking that addiction had caused a dependence on surrogates that had wrecked her health. She was here in this hospital because of all that. Was that why he was here? Did he feel in the least little way to blame?

Now though, she had won her way back to from the darkness; she felt strong and clean, self-reliant and free. And she looked at Carlyle with new eyes. There he lounged, sleek and self-indulgent, taking her continued devotion for granted. What had she seen to love all these years ago?

"He's the up and coming man, you know. I'm lucky to get an interview with him. I hear he's in line for a top job here if he cares to take it. There are rumours the PM is interested. It says in *The Financial Times*…"

Meg listened to him sadly. He had come out of his way to visit her. It was years since they had last met. He imagined he loved her still but he did not see her or know her at all. To him she was a past mistress set aside for the furtherance of his career, a trifle to be looked at now and then like a trophy in a cabinet, a necessary adjunct to his own self-esteem.

What had happened to them in the intervening years? Once he had seemed to have so much more intelligence and savoir-faire than she. Meg had admired him, been guided by him, adored him. Now he seemed to have as much substance as a rag-doll.

"We are the hollow men..."

He was still pontificating about his big business in America when the nurse came to call Meg to lunch. As he briefly kissed her good-bye his mind was already on his journey to the airport.

He handed her *The Financial Times* as he left.

"Here. You can read about the merger in this," he said. "I've finished with it."

AFTER lunch Meg lay in the garden. A plane droned overhead on the flight path to America. Bees buzzed in the carnations and the honeysuckle drowsed in the heat. Her head drooped on to Carlyle's pink pages.

She could not be bothered reading them but they made a good pillow – his soft present.

CHRISTMAS DINNER

IT was a beautiful goose. It fitted neatly into the oven and sat on its wire rack oozing succulent juices. Christmas dinner was going to be good. Everything was ready at the right time and done to perfection potatoes white and floury, gravy rich, Brussels sprouts green and firm.

It was, you may say, satisfactory.

Mary had had the flu since the beginning of the school holidays but, determined not to have the family Christmas spoiled, she had made a big effort to appear normal on Christmas Day and almost succeeded in ignoring the persistent symptoms.

Meanwhile, Tom had used all his artistry to lay the table. The living-room was transformed. Candles and holly and red mats covered the lace cloth. Glittering glasses and crackers of silver-blue and green-gold foil reflected back the mellow light.

"It's been worth the effort," she thought, happily glancing round at them, her husband opposite and the two boys to right and left. "We have made something beautiful."

For about five minutes it was perfect and then Bobby began to wilt with adolescent self-pity. He said he had a headache; his head was so sore he could not bear the light. He put on a pair of sunglasses and drooped over his plate, a death's head at the feast in a Motorhead T-shirt, so sorry for himself that he made sympathy impossible. Eventually he had to be excused to go and lie on the sofa. His goose went back in the hot drawer.

For a short while longer the dinner continued, not too blighted by his absence. Wee Sandy guzzled happily, fetched more crackers and played with hats and mottoes until the martyred voice from the sofa reminded him that he was missing the *Paul Daniels Show* on TV.

And that, Mary reflected later, was where she had made the mistake. She should have vetoed TV and yet she had promised to have dinner ready earlier so that Sandy could watch his favourite conjurer. She wavered and the moment was gone. The *Magic Show* was turned on and the magic was lost. Atmosphere died in the room with the turn of the switch.

Only she and Tom were left at the lovely table. They continued the meal, telling each other how good it was, drinking each other's health but when the time came for the ritual of the blazing pudding it did not seem to be the right time any more. It was all there waiting, but exhaustion and the need for a cup of coffee overtook her so the pudding was postponed. Perhaps in a little while they would be able to retrieve the atmosphere. Perhaps it could still be as in other years, before Tom's problems made life so unpredictable.

She thought wistfully of past Christmases when the children were small enough to be tucked away in bed by seven o'clock, when television did not dominate the evening, when they could put on a dreamy record and sit on the rug by the fire, sipping wine, making love.

And then Tom announced that he was going to phone his mother, poor old soul, to wish her a Merry Christmas. Off he went with a pocketful of change for the phone box.

"Now, don't you touch the dishes," he said. "That's my job. You did all the cooking."

Thankfully, Mary agreed. Flu symptoms were crawling back.

It was a relief to leave the broken carcase and the greasy plates for someone else to clear up. The boys were now watching James Bond and for a while she followed his antics with them. Bobby's head had made a truly remarkable recovery and he ate his warmed-up goose with relish.

Time passed and Tom did not come back.

Unease gripped her stomach.

He wouldn't have abandoned them, tonight of all nights, to go to the pub, would he? She tried to look calm and unconcerned for the boys' sake but worry made her restless. She paced about, clearing the table, burning cracker debris, poking the fire and finally, hardly aware of what she was doing, she attacked the stacks of dirty dishes and pots.

Far too soon they were all clean and now there was nothing to do until the film ended, when, falsely cheerful, she suggested they go for a walk.

"Where's Dad?" asked Sandy.

"Oh, he went to phone his Mum. He must have got held up," she said, stress showing through the cracks in her offhandedness.

They slid down the frosty hill, through the deserted streets, playing with Christmas torches, quoting Dylan Thomas, gazing at the stars. Of course there was nobody at all near the row of phone-boxes in the empty square.

"Dad's not there."

"Perhaps he has gone home another way."

"Perhaps he'll be there when we get back."

But of course he wasn't.

"Can we have pudding now, Mum?

"Yes. I don't suppose we can wait any longer," she replied and, sick with the disgust of disappointment, she reheated the pudding, flamed the brandy, dimmed the lights and tried pathetically to capture a little of the small ritual that had meant so much to them each Christmas past before Tom had changed.

She watched them spoon the pudding, eagerly looking for treasure.

One boy got a wrapped sixpence for wealth, the other her wedding ring for happiness as they were meant to. But she took nothing herself.

Nothing could have induced a piece of that pudding down her aching throat.

When the boys were in bed she stood alone in the kitchen, brooding bitterly.

The slob *had* abandoned them. It was unbelievable. What had been the use of all her work, all the effort in trying to create the perfect family celebration when he had cared so little for them that he had preferred to slither off to the pub tonight of all nights, the creep!

Black, burning resentment and rage soured her. *Goodwill to all men!* Ha!

She caught sight of his bonnet lying on a chair. It was so very much his – a brown corduroy cap with a high front and a stiff peak. All the bitterness for the spoiled Christmas, all the festering misery and desolation, all her incredulity at his desertion fastened on the bonnet.

With loathing Mary carried it at arm's length to the living-room fire and placed it on the hot coals. Then she sat quietly with hands folded in her lap and gazed into the flames. The cap lay there defencelessly for some moments, then flames burst through the crown. Smoke poured up the chimney, creaming and curling, until gradually the whole hat, brim and rim and peak, was consumed.

When he arrived home at last, bleary and stupid and guilty, the ash-white skeleton of the cap still remained, fragile as a cobweb on the dying embers of the fire.

THE WASTE

THE caravan was a shock to Marion. She had not expected a de luxe model but this! She got out of the car and clambered stiffly over a rusty bed-frame tied with binder-twine.

The van's surroundings were unique for a start. It stood on two flat tyres inside a World War Two gun emplacement on a headland above a desolate shore. Green turf sloped around at roof level, sheltering it from the Atlantic winds and giving it total privacy. Grey concrete bunkers hid the view from the windows, ugly and claustrophobic but practical in that bleak landscape. The wrecks of other wind-shattered caravans testified to that.

She noticed firewood in one bunker and a smell of cats. Sheep droppings too. They must have got over the bedstead and she wondered how while she unlocked the door.

Her first sight of the outer van had destroyed all her expectations of comfort so she was agreeably surprised by the interior. Though the paint was dull, the cushions shabby and the worn floor gritty with blown sand, the challenge of making it her home was a prospect that took her mind away from the troubles she had come so far to escape. Duncan would have hated this, she thought with pleasure. He'll have made for the nearest hotel on the star chart.

The stovepipe's chimney lay on the floor. It had to be fitted before a fire could be lit. Marion grew hot and exasperated wrestling with it before she discovered the technique and it slid in with a rusty squeak. She had done it by herself. No man had come to her aid while she stood helplessly by.

She climbed off the bunker and proceeded to stoke the stove. The gas cooker posed no problems and soon her box of groceries was unpacked; bacon was sizzling in the pan and she had a mug of coffee by a blazing fire.

From the roof of the caravan she had seen over the bunker walls to the great grey beach that lay open to the western ocean. The tide was going down with the sun and long-legged birds poked busily in the sand. The rear windows looked over the bedstead through the sheltered gap in the wall to a range of mountains purple in the sunset.

Marion felt better. Perhaps this would do after all. Perhaps she could heal herself in the solitude of this empty land.

Once this place had swarmed with men trained to anger; men intent on killing. The huge gun that once stood in this green circle would have swivelled its eye to and fro watching the sea. Duncan used to roll his eyes when he was angry. Like a mad bull.

The soldiers had left. The landscape was defenceless now and ruined by their memories. It was scarred by the foundations of Nissen huts and broken walls. Derelict watchtowers grinned at the sea. Each croft bore its war wound and dealt with it according to the owners's ingenuity.

Broken gables sheltered henhouses; cows were penned in roofless concrete honeycombs. There were caravans everywhere and empty staring houses.

Marion brooded.

"I am like this countryside wrecked by the violence of men, like the rubbish washed up on the shore down there. I'll rot if I don't watch out. .... Oh, now I'm talking morbid rubbish! Get a grip, girl!"

She made another cup of coffee and poked a stick into the fire. It was wonderful not having to bother about anyone but herself, not having to wonder whether it pleased Duncan that she wanted to stay by the fire.

Marriage was a cage and she had broken her spirit on the bars. Had it been a trap for Duncan too? She remembered the day that she had become aware of his affaire with her best friend; the moment was frozen like a snapshot: she at the kitchen door, they gazing deep into each other's eyes. Then they had turned and seen her with the knowledge in her eyes and nothing had been the same again.

"Why did I not walk out on them there and then? I gained nothing by staying. We tried so hard to put a respectable face on things to cover it all up – camouflage like this gun site and underneath we were at war the whole time. I felt so betrayed, so vindictive. I took my revenge in so many subtle ways and Duncan defended himself with brutality."

Why did he not leave? He was concerned with preserving appearances too – his job, his mistress's good name. God! The frustration and the hypocrisy! That's why we all took to drink. Well, *we* took to drink; Betty had her valium. We were out of our minds most of the time. Remember the nightmares when you would see your clenched fingers splitting into overlapping shells of raw meat like the ruffled feathers of a bird. Remember standing at the gable-end, screaming and screaming into the howling of the wind. Remember the nights when Duncan would pace the floor up and down, to and fro and you, silly with lack of sleep, would yell at him until he hit you and knocked you, sobbing on the bed."

Marion realised that she was shaking. The fire was low; the caravan was dark. She filled a bottle and huddled under her duvet, shivering with the stress of remembered misery. A lighthouse flashed a pinprick in the dark and she watched it two flashes and a long pause, two flashes and a long pause till the monotony relaxed her and, comforted, she slept.

NEXT morning she was awakened by sunlight and the clinking of bottles.

"Duncan!" She thought, until she remembered she was safe.

In the next gun emplacement was a portakabin fitted up as a laboratory. A haphazard clutter of reagent bottles, winchesters and buckets surrounded it. Two scientists were busy doing something with samples of liquid and test tubes. They looked at her with interest when she came to the tap to fill her kettle and said, "Good morning."

She felt their admiration and realised that maybe she was not as destroyed as she had thought. Their greeting warmed her; their inscrutable business roused her curiosity. She wished she had the nerve to ask them what they were doing, and why, but she felt shy and went back inside to boil her kettle for breakfast.

"I'll go down to the shore after I've tidied up. I'll collect more driftwood and watch the birds. Maybe I'll paddle in the sea."

The days went by. Nobody else came up the broken road that ended at the portakabin. Marion ate sparingly, walked a good deal and even swam in the shockingly cold sea. At the back of the bunker she discovered cartoons of Hitler with a hammer at his head and a sickle at his throat. He was surrounded by sexy drawings of women, all bosoms and high heels.

"Duncan was a soldier once. Perhaps the idea that man is the enemy and woman the lust object never leaves you. He treated me with contempt and resented me having a mind of my own. He sneered at my ideas long before he went off with Betty. I wonder if he sneered at her. But he was always jealous of other men always wary of competition. Poor Duncan!"

She realised that this was the first time she had felt sympathy for the man for a long, long time. Perhaps the ruined landscape was bringing its own healing to her. She wanted to stay on in this lonely peninsula forever, tucked away from the storms in her emasculated mound.

The grocer's van came to the road end each week and she made stilted conversation there with the crofters' wives. They knew her cousin who had lent her the caravan but they were polite and did not intrude on her privacy beyond offering eggs and milk. Sometimes she collected these; sometimes a boy left them inside the bed-frame gate.

Life drifted on and nobody bothered her. She began to draw and paint again, stiffly at first but with increasing confidence. She learned the names of the flowers and birds, using the yellowing reference books on the caravan shelves.

Gradually the van began to be home. It filled up with curious pebbles, interesting pieces of driftwood too good to burn. The woodpile was always in a healthy state and she found she could burn the dry peat turf fringing the sand dunes.

The scientists became friendly. She would give them coffee when they arrived to take their marine samples. Marion watched them do it and one day they let her help. It was easy. She felt proud that she could cope.

Duncan had fed his ego by keeping her in her place. He had exerted mastery by insisting on her female futility. Her confidence had become so eroded that she felt everyone must despise her. These men did not sneer.

"It's a nuisance coming out here every week," they said. "Perhaps we could give you a job." The possibility was there.

Marion now felt life had some hope to offer. She began to feel that she was a worthwhile person; she was getting to know herself and her personality was unfolding.

Shyly at first, she began to speak to the other women and greet any locals she met by name. They liked her. She became welcome in their houses.

The queer landscape had restored her soul – no green pastures and quiet waters here but a thin strip of machair between barren moor and the sucking, surging sea, a strip of machair made ugly by man's dereliction and yet it had made her a whole woman again.

ONE morning Marion set out to draw the lighthouse. She walked along the cliffs with confidence, the wind in her hair. She noted the names of the birds she passed and the flowers in the grass – tormentil, self-heal, lady's slipper. She peered over the edge to watch a tenement of guillemots nesting precariously and laughed with delight at the absurdity of such crowded quarters in a place so empty and free. She saw a seal bobbing at the end of a reef and cormorants hanging out their wings to dry and she strode along the edge, strong and careless.

"I'm free. I am myself and I'm absolutely free."

Then her foot slipped and horrified, she watched the boulder she had dislodged tumble over and over in the empty air, spinning down the black cliff to make a tiny splash in the greedy surge far below.

Sick, she thought, "If that had been me falling just when everything is beginning again, what a waste!"

And she turned away from the dangerous edge, back to the caravan and security.

As she climbed over the bedstead, Duncan stepped out of the bunker to meet her.

THE BAD STEP

"I'M not ready for it, Kate."

"Of course you are. You just put your boots in the crack and you don't look down. It's not difficult, Anne. It just needs nerve."

Anne knew that she did not have much nerve but she knew too there was no way back. It was not just Kate's challenge she had to meet. She had to make the attempt now or despise herself.

"Well, as long as you think I am up to it . . . but you'll have to talk me across. I'm scared stiff."

They had walked to Coruisk from Sligachan, eight miles through the glen, then over Druim Hain and down the narrow defile to the sea: Kate judged it was now time to tackle the Bad Step but Anne had her doubts.

Someone had made a bothy under an overhanging ledge, filling the narrow space with sea-washed boards and dried heather and building up a neat drystone wall – a snug billet for a benighted walker. "*SKID ROW*" was scratched at its entrance.

Even as they were laughing at the name, dread was gripping Anne's gut. It was as bad as going to the dentist before a driving test. Ahead of them was the Bad Step, far too near a bulging outcrop of gabbro, naked mountain obliterating the track. The only way to negotiate it was to edge across the slant crack in its ice-smoothed surface. The path taking up again on either side looked laughably simple.

Kate strode forward confidently.

"I'll never do it, Kate," Anne called, panic-stricken.

"Of course you will. Keep calm. Don't tell yourself you can't. Say, We *will* do it."

Will-power that's what I need, Anne thought. *Why am I doing this anyway? Why do I need to prove myself like this? Will I be any better for achieving it? Won't I just have to meet a bigger and more dangerous challenge next time?*

Kate was already on the rock, hands spread.

"Come on. Don't think about it. Do it."

"Yes, I know. Get your boots in the crack and don't look down."

Anne stood for a last precious minute on the lovely soft peat before committing herself to the rock. The crack was filled with small plants – dwarf lovage, roseroot, herb robert – sheltered in their niche from the weather but stunted by the boots of passing climbers. The crevice tilted alarmingly down. It curved over a bulge and seemed to drop straight into the sea.

Anne felt sick and desperate. She could see Kate's red nylon rucksack moving crabwise out of the corner of her eye. She dared not look further.

I wish this abominable crack did not slope down. I wouldn't be so scared if we were climbing away from the sea. We should have tackled it from the other side for my first time. I bet Kate didn't feel so good her first time either. I wish I felt as confident as she looks.

"Come on, Anne, you're doing fine. Keep edging along."

"Okay! I'm edging. I'm edging!

She called back cheerily, but what she thought was: *Oh God! This is an ordeal. It's too much for me. I should never have let myself in for it.*

"Okay! I'm coming slow but sure I'm . . . Oh, my God! Oh, Kate! Oh No! Look out! KATE!" Kate, the expert, had slipped.

Somehow the unthinkable was happening. It was Kate who had taken the bad step.

She had missed her footing and her boots were slithering down the smoothed slab, hopelessly trying for a grip.

Anne, spread frozen on the slab, stared into the eyes of her friend, stared at her nails clawing for a hold on the hostile rock, stared as she slid down the overhang into sheer air and was gone. Her eyes strained at emptiness but her ears were full of Kate's falling wail and the splash as her body hit the sea.

What'll I do? What'll I do? Oh help! Help! Anne's transfixed horror and disbelief seemed to last for eternity, her mind in cold storage but her feet were already turning back off the rock on to the steep slope of heather and scree.

There must be a way down. There has to be. I'll never make it in time. Oh God, help me. Please. Please!

Scrambling and sliding, sending stones crashing in front of her, tearing at heather roots to brake her descent, Anne somehow made it as near the water's edge as she could. Round the bulge of the Bad Step she could see Kate in the water, struggling to keep herself afloat but her boots were heavy and her pack was pushing her face forward into the water. She was a weak swimmer at the best of times.

"Kate!" Anne screamed. "Take off your pack. Hold it in front of you, Kate! Take off your pack! Use it as a float. Hold on. I'm coming."

The water was clear, green, attractive, the bottom free of rocks and weed, an idyllic spot for a swim, a dive even, on another day in other circumstances. Anne had not hesitated. Even as she was calling to Kate she was tearing off her haversack, her boots and her jersey.

There was no shore. The mountain slid into the sea sheer as the side of a tank. No warm pool water here.

Put all your life-saving lessons to the test, she thought. *You'll need them all. Swim for your life and hers.*

Lying in the cold green salty water, shooting along, Anne had a surprising burst of confidence. She felt almost light-hearted.

I can do this. I'm in my element now. Better not speak too soon, though . . ..

"Kate! Can you hear me? I'm coming to help you. Don't try to grab me. NO! Look, Kate, I can't rescue you if you hold me. Let *me* hold you. Relax. Trust me. That's it. Good, girl. Put your head back. Look at the sky.

"That's right. Now I'll take the strap of your bag and tow you for a bit. Can you kick with your legs?

"Okay? Here we go . . ."

Oh God! Give me strength. This water's cold and she's heavy. I've never towed anyone with boots on before. Please don't let us drown. . . Sea slipping past my ear, one eye at the horizon, rocks sliding by far too slowly grey boulders, orange lichen, brown seaweed my own gasping breath kick and glide, kick and glide. . . .

"Don't struggle, Kate! Hold on!"

I'm tiring. Water's washing over my face. I must keep going just a few metres now. Give me strength. Kick and glide kick and – we've grounded! I scraped bottom. Oh thank you! Thank you!

"Kate, We're ashore!"

Anne crawled up the tiny beach, dragging Kate's sagging, dripping weight. They collapsed, limp as tidewrack on the sickle of sand.

"Kate, you're okay now. We're safe."

But we're not. The troubles are only beginning. I'll have to do something quick or we'll both get hypothermia. I'll have to go and get my rucksack; there's a survival bag in it. And I need my boots. . .

"Kate, I'm going for my things. No. It's all right; I won't be long. Don't give up on me. I'll soon have us warm again."

Anne's own fingers were bone-white with cold but adrenalin sent her back into the sea to swim to the edge of the Bad Step where she had scattered her belongings. It was quicker than scrambling over stones and heather in bare feet.

Thankfully, she retrieved her rucksack and, tearing off her wet shirt pulled on a dry jersey and anorak. As she laced her boots she could see poor Kate sprawled small and stranded like jetsam from the tide.

I must get back. She'll die of cold. At least she's breathing.

Her boots thudded the rhythm of her thoughts along the track and down to the sand. In the pocket she never used was the survival bag, elastoplast and a whistle; often these precautions had seemed self-consciously prudent and they had embarrassed her slightly. Now the bag was life itself for Kate. But before she could put it into use Anne noticed something else.

Oh no! The tide 's turned. We'll have to move. But where? I know! If I have to move her anyway I could get her up to that bothy. It's not very far. She'd be out of the wind once the sun goes down.

She knelt by her friend. Kate was conscious but badly shocked and shivering. There was a livid bump on her head and her left ankle was askew.

"Kate, listen. We'll have to move from here. Can you hop a bit if I half-carry you? We'll go up to that Skid Row place for shelter."

Kate nodded feebly. Wrapping the thermal sheet round her and taking one arm over her shoulder, Anne dragged her upright and they staggered lopsidedly up the rock slabs. The gabbro looked like liver that had been dropped in grit but it gave good grip to their boots. Anne lugged her up to the track, down the boggy defile and at last pushed her up and into the narrow cave mouth. They both collapsed on the wiry heather floor.

"Right, Kate. Let's get you into your sack. Like a parcel."

Anne was worn out. Her muscles were aching and sweat was breaking out in her hair. The effort of getting Kate into the bag in such a confined space nearly finished her. She could not get into the narrow kist alongside her and had to reach in bent double. Stones pressed agonisingly into her knees. She did not know whether to weep or curse and did both.

Once Kate was bedded on the dry heather Anne collapsed again flat out, legs dangling over the lip of the cave mouth. Relaxing was blissful agony and far too brief.

"Oh hell! I'll have to go back and get my rucksack before the tide does."

She struggled to her feet again. Her knees felt like water and reaction was setting in. She realised she was trembling.

Down at the beach, as she looped her pack over her shoulder, she noticed something bobbing close to the shore. It was Kate's waterlogged rucksack. Maybe something had survived. She fished it out with a piece of driftwood. Chocolate, peanuts, a dead phone and Kate's survival bag. Oh wonderful! She could make a sort of tent for herself cut holes in the top and walk about in it.

SKID ROW felt like home when she returned.

Pity we can't have a fire. Next time I'll carry matches. Next time I'll have a mobile too. Next time! What am I saying?

Kate was white and quiet, half-dozing. Was it all right to let her do that? Probably the best thing. She was conserving energy and warmth. At least she was breathing.

Anne gave herself a whole bar of chocolate and drank some hot black coffee. Her teeth chattered on the rim of the cup but she felt cocooned and warm. Soon she would have to try for help but that could wait. This time of rest and food was hers. Still, the thought of what she must do gave her no peace. It had seemed like a good idea to take their walk when the hills were quiet, when the tourists had departed, when there were no day trippers from the boats. Now she scanned the hillsides for the sight of a woolly bonnet. In vain.

*Will it be safe to leave Kate? Will it be safe not to? I'll just have to go. I must get help. Oh! I **wish** somebody would come. It's eight miles to Sligachan. Eight miles!*

It can't be helped. I'm not going over the Bad Step. Not now, not ever. I'd better get going before the adrenalin wears out .

"Kate, can you hear me? I'm going to get help. It'll take a good while but don't worry. You'll be rescued. Just stay there now and take it easy. Don't give up on me, Kate. Hang on."

With a sob in her voice, Anne walked away.

Round the end of Loch Coruisk and up the side of the burn. Head down, foot forward, bring up the other one. Make yourself do it. Plod on.

I'm tired . I'll never make it. Perhaps I should have stayed. What if she dies alone! Oh, God, please send someone, please. . . .

"I to the hills will lift mine eyes from whence doth come mine aid. . . "

From whence doth come mine aid. . . from whence doth come mine aid . . . a mindless rhythm from childhood to the squelch and thud of her boots.

Every few minutes Anne collapsed, taking great gulps of air, relaxing utterly, then forcing herself to get up and stagger on.

Once over the ridge the worst will be past. I hate climbing hills. I'll never climb another one as long as I live.! I hope that's not prophetic.

Oh, God, send someone send someone send someone, **please.** *From whence doth come..from whence doth come ...from whence?*

The horizon was foreshortening as she hauled herself up the convex slope from one cairn to the next. The cairns marked the track across the bare ice-scoured rock. They played tricks with her, mocked her; always there was another one beyond. She was on all fours now. Her breath was tearing her throat raw. She staggered a few more feet and some more and then collapsed.

Over her rasping breath she heard a rock clatter.

A couple of walkers were coming over the top of the pass towards her. "Oh help!" she gasped. "Help us, please."

NO FOOL LIKE AN OLD FOOL

"MAM! *MAM!* The gerbils have had babies!" I opened one eye. The clock stared back at me. Six thirty a.m.

"They can't have. They're males. Go back to bed."

I turned over, groaning. The boys were having me on. It was April the First. Well, they wouldn't catch me out with that one.

I hated April 1st, All Fools' Day. As a mother and a primary school teacher it was the particular day in the year when I was at the butt-end of drawing-pins on chairs, chalk marks on backs, silly messages. I admit I had revenged myself now and then by sending the perpetrators to the science lab. in the secondary block for a long stand or a sharp retort but usually I just kept my wits about me and longed for noon. Folk belief decreed the joke rebounded on the joker after midday.

"Mam! Mam! It's TRUE! Come and see! Mam, you have to. We don't know what to do."

The gerbils lived in a tank downstairs – at that time in the morning a stair too far.

"Go away. It's April Fools'. I'm not falling for that one."

"Mam! We're not fooling. Please come and see." My elder son had now added his voice to the chorus.

I dragged on my dressing-gown and, grumpy and barefoot, I tramped down to the living-room. Scott grabbed my arm in his urgency.

"Look! Look! In there. There's a nest. Dangermouse has had babies and Penfold is *eating* them!"

His voice rose to a shriek.

I peered into the tank. Among the shredded paper and chewed up toilet rolls I could just make out some pinkish-purple blobs.

"Oh, very good! Well done, but you're still not fooling me. They're PLASTICINE!"

"MAM!"

And then I saw one move . . . *It had only three legs.*

THE GIRL AT DARROCH

NONE of this would have happened if it had not been for the gerbils.

My son had got a pair of them – two males, carefully chosen – but by April Fools' Day the guaranteed bachelors had produced a litter of eight and in a fortnight they were weaned. I was at my wits' end.

Fortunately my cousin, Marion came to the rescue. She lived across the water in Lower Drasdale, my childhood home, and she had no difficulty in finding takers for our superfluous brood.

One day then I drove across to Drasdale with the baby gerbils rustling in a box of torn paper on the back seat.

Now, although Lower Drasdale is only fifty miles from my present home and much less if you are a crow, it had ceased to exist for me once my parents moved away. I do not believe in retracing my steps to indulge in nostalgia. If a place belongs to my past that is where it will remain unless there is some special reason for returning. I had had a happy childhood and my memories were clear and brilliant. I had no wish to fog them with disillusionment.

I was to deliver the gerbils to a house called Darroch, which I had known intimately as a child. Next door to my old home and separated from it only by a field, I had made free of it and had always been made welcome there. It was an old manse, strongly built and pleasantly proportioned, set back from the road among aged rook-filled trees. The garden and glebe fields had lain fallow for decades and the place was a wilderness of rank grass and wild daffodils. Over the garden wall was a historic ruined church, ivy-covered, surrounded by haphazard grave-stones and at the back were substantial steadings belonging to the age when the minister had the glebe farm to run as well as his parish.

In my childhood a very old man had lived there with his two house-keepers, spinster sisters. His own family seldom visited and my company was welcomed. I could visualize it all – the stone flags in the scullery, the Daniell prints in the sombre hall, the wooden coat-stand where the old man's ecclesiastical hat and cloak hung in rusty, dusty disuse long after he had died.

Long after he had died we still kept the key at our house because the family visited the property only rarely and did nothing with it. During my school holidays I would let myself in to ramble about, exploring the nurseries, the attics and best of all, the library. The house was silted up with the possessions of generations.

Darroch enchanted me. I was a solitary creature by choice and I spent hours there indulging in fancies while the dusk crept in from the grave-yard trees and I remained oblivious to my loneliness.

Over the years the house gently decayed. Damp sprang through the roof; mildew spotted the valuable books. A village woman was engaged to dust and clean occasionally and then I would accompany her because she found it too spooky on her own.

I never found Darroch eerie. I felt sad for it, angry at those who neglected it. I wanted to protect it, to possess it but rather it possessed me. I had nothing but my love for it; those who had the money for its upkeep were eccentrically indifferent to their property. And then my parents moved to another job, another village. I went to university, grew up, married and left my childhood country in the land of memory, the scenery of dreams.

Until now.

As I approached my destination my apprehension grew. I was afraid of what I would find and I braced myself for changes.

I had never driven up to the door before. Always I had walked up the cobbled lane between lichen-crusty drystane dykes under the ragged hawthorns.

Now the home park over the wall was a sea of mud, dotted with makeshift jumps for ponies.

The gaps in the dyke were stuffed with tangled rylock and battered oil drums but little else had changed. There were bright curtains at the shining windows and the door had new paint but the garden was a jungle and the gravel still full of weeds.

I stood gazing past the trees and over the burn to the familiar hills. I could feel the place in every cell of my being. This was where I belonged. I knew the stones in the water and the moss in the grass where the first flowers grew. I knew what was behind and beyond with an intensity that no time could dispel. I was lost in my awareness of it all as I stood by the car.

A young woman was standing on the gravel waiting for me to come out of my reverie. She had merry brown eyes and curly hair and I liked her on sight.

"You were miles away," she said. "You must be Marnie with the gerbils."

"That's right. I've brought them. And you must be Jan. Marion often speaks about you. You are wrong though – I wasn't miles away. I was right here but in another time. It's a very strange experience coming back after so many years and finding the place so unchanged."

"I liked Darroch the way I found it and I want to keep it that way. I'm not a great one for needing to make my mark on places so I just fixed up the worst of the dilapidation. You'll find changes round in the steading though. The ponies are there."

"Changes for the better, I'm sure. It's good to see the buildings being used again."

"Come on in. We'll talk better over a coffee. I'll show you round later. Will the gerbils be all right if we leave them for a little while? Jim isn't home from school yet."

Still talking, she led the way through the old iron gates to the back door and I followed, gazing around. The scullery, of course, had been modernised with vinyl on the floor and gleaming equipment, but the cosy atmosphere remained in the housekeepers' room and I settled down by the familiar fireplace and accepted a mug of coffee from Jan with pleasure.

We smiled at each other.

"It's lovely to be back," I said. "It's like coming home. I know this place so well. I suppose Marion told you I grew up here – well – next door really but I was back and fore all the time. I know every nook and cranny in the bank of the burn from its mouth to its source. I often visited the old folk who lived here and after they had gone I used to trespass quite freely. Darroch lay derelict for years. It must have been in an awful state when you bought it. Tell me, did you buy the contents of the house or was there a sale?"

"There was a sale of sorts. The best things went away to auction but we got a great deal of stuff with the house – vast amounts of rubbish mostly."

"I wish I had known you when you were clearing it out. It would have been fascinating. Was there a jigsaw with lilacs on it? I used to play with it when my mother visited. It had big wooden lugs and I thought the flowers were beautiful. And did they sell the book with *'the receipe for the cure of the scarlett spottifs'*?"

Jan laughed. "Yes and no. The jigsaw is still there, lugs and lilac and all, but the recipe book was valuable and it went to the sale."

"I bet it was valuable. I wonder what they did with the money."

"Well, they didn't spend much of it on this place. That's certain. It was heading for dereliction when we bought it. I'm so glad we did."

"I'm very glad you did too."

The talk drifted this way and that. I felt completely relaxed in Jan's company, as if we were old friends. I sensed she felt the same but once or twice I caught her looking at me intently, a puzzled line between her brows.

At last she said, "You know, it's queer but I get the feeling that I know you quite well but we have never met before, have we?"

"Not unless in a previous existence." And we both laughed.

"Talking of ghosts," I went on, "have you seen any? When the old man lived here he used to claim that he saw a lady in a long dress in the corridor at the top of the stair. And he was a minister of the Kirk. He used to pray for her."

Jan suddenly looked uneasy. She frowned and poked the fire before she spoke.

"Well, actually, I *have* seen a ghost. At least I think I have. I'm not sure. It's all too strange. She is not a conventional wraith in a long dress. I don't believe in that sort of thing. But I have seen – och – it's too silly!"

"Go on! Tell me."

"Well, sometimes I see a young girl around the place and there is nobody living in the village that fits her description. I've asked. She's quite ordinary – tall, dressed in a tartan skirt and a rather skimpy jersey and her hair is done in pigtails.

"There's nothing ghostly about her at all, except that one minute I see her, the next she's gone.

"To begin with I used to see her outside – across the burn by the ruined cottages or poking about in the graveyard and then I began to see her around the garden.

"I was very indignant to begin with. She acted as if the place belonged to her."

"Have you spoken to her?"

"Well, yes. I came in one day from the garden and there she was in the corridor. You know how dark it is in there and I was dazzled by the sunlight. I asked her what she wanted but she gazed right past me. I turned to see what she was staring at and when I looked back she was gone. She simply wasn't there.

"Then I came across her another day curled up in the library reading an old book. At least I thought I saw her. When I switched on the light the chair was empty.

"And sometimes I hear singing. It's funny you should have mentioned that wooden jigsaw. I heard crooning up in the attics one day and went up to investigate. That was the day I noticed the jigsaw."

"Does she spook you?"

"No. I can't say that she does.

"The singing is a bit eerie at times but if she is the spirit of the place she's a kindly one."

"Has anyone else seen her?"

"No. That's the strangest thing. Nobody else has. I don't really believe in the supernatural so I don't talk about it much. Once I discovered she was nobody living locally I stopped mentioning her. It's quite a relief to get it off my chest to you."

"It's fascinating! I never felt the slightest aura of ghostliness in this house all the time I visited it, despite its closeness to the cemetery. I just didn't expect to see anything – but then – neither did you!

The door banged against the wall with terrifying velocity. I yelled and sprang out of my chair.

Jan laughed. "It's only Jim back from school."

"Mum, is that the lady with the gerbils? OH, MUM, can I see them? Can I see them?"

There was no more talk of ghosts after that.

I left Darroch in the evening promising to return soon. I felt soaringly happy and sang all the way home. My rapport with the old place had been strengthened and renewed through Jan and I looked forward to many returns.

I have been back several times since then and my welcome is assured.

One June morning recently Jan and I were having our coffee on the seat by the front door. I was lying with my eyes shut against the sun, dreamy with the scent of briar roses on the warm sandstone at my back, humming contentedly under my breath, when Jan said: "Marnie, do you remember your first visit – how I told you about the girl I used to see wandering about the place? Well, you know, it's a funny thing but I have never seen her since."

"I should think that was a relief. You must be glad to be rid of her," I said drowsily.

"No, seriously. I have never seen or heard of her since and I'd almost forgotten her until today but that tune you were humming just now was the one I heard her singing up in the attics the day I found the jigsaw – *your* jigsaw – with the flowers on it. It's queer, isn't it, that I've never seen or heard that girl again since the day you came – until now?"

I could feel cold prickles breaking out on my skin.

"When I was a girl," I said slowly, "I usually wore a tartan skirt and a jersey and my hair was invariably in pigtails. Are you thinking what I'm thinking, that the ghost you saw was me?"

We stared at each other, wide-eyed and wondering.

Who else could it have been?

132

WESTERN ISLAND

When the wild geese fly for the winter
I think of my Western island;
when the snowclouds smother the rainbow
and the sea's a welter of foam;
when the west wind sobs in the chimney
and flattens the moorland grasses
and the fuschia tassels stepdance
in the hedges around my home.
When the stormclouds batter the hillsides
I think of my Western island
where the breakers boom in the caverns
and thunder and hiss on the shore;
when the spindrift whirls on the surface
of the wind-whipped, cowering water
and the smoke blows back to the fireside
and the rain creeps under the door.
When the swans are arrowing southwards
I think of a winter island
for the summer there is fragile
with a beauty as soft as rain.
And I'll go down to the ferry
where the road slides under the water
then wanders around my island
and stops at my home again.

MRS MILLER

I REMEMBER sitting one day on the bare kitchen table in the School-house at Lochcarron to be out of the way while Mrs Miller put a skin on the linoleum. She was never done polishing. Folk walked warily where Mrs Miller knelt. I was trying to read *Jock o' Hazeldean* from a wee green poetry book:

A chain of gold ye shall not lack
Nor braid to bind your hair,
Nor mettled hound, nor managed hawk,
Nor palfrey fresh and fair

"What's a palfrey?" I asked.

I must have been pretty small at the time. The kitchen was big and I was far off the ground. I had managed all the other words and even the sense of the poem, except that I had pictured the hound as metalled, hung about with metal trappings like chains of gold. Mrs Miller had no idea what a palfrey was, although no doubt, she would have known plenty about ponies. She was the matriarch of the local tinkers.

In those days, just after the Second World War, they still had many of their old ways of life left to them. Her husband, whom she always called Laochan, was a skilled tinsmith. He made the pails we all needed to carry our milk and Mrs Miller now and again made a round with a clutch of shiny newly tinned pails, their lids fitting like snug silk. He would mend things too and he once riveted my mother's big mixing bowl so that it was as good as ever.

The Millers had a proper place in the community and were treated with dignity and respect although "tinks" in general were viewed with suspicion and a good deal of ribaldry.

Lochcarron was a focal point for these travelling people although there were families based on Garve, Plockton, Skye and Gairloch too, all inter-related. Dingwall, the county town, had its own urban tribes, who dealt in scrap. They would arrive from the east on speedy flat carts, rubber-tyred and pulled by fast-trotting ponies. The women would be wrapped about in plaid shawls, sometimes with a baby hidden in the folds and when they set up camp they sheltered in tents of hooped hazel covered with tarpaulins.

One of their favourite places was on the steeply wooded sides of the burn on Kishorn Hill. The village called their encampment Beverley Hills and the name became even more enjoyed in its irony when they began to turn their tents into tarred and felted huts to seek a more settled way of life.

The Millers, however, got a council house – one of the 'New Houses' that went up after the war.

Mrs Miller was a fanatical housewife. She polished and cleaned and shone with true Romany zeal. Her house was so spotless that even the snootiest village gossip had nothing to criticise. And she came to help my mother whose health was frail throughout most of my childhood.

She could not help me with the palfrey but she could regale me with wonderful tales of the little green men that lived in the hollow hills and all my life *Jock o' Hazeldean* has remained for me a magical tale of the greenwood with little green men watching through the fronds.

Mrs Miller was Mrs Malaprop personified. She loved using high-falutin' words and managed always to put her own individual stamp on them. In the days before electricity came marching over the hills, when we all had Tilley lamps, she went to Kenny Stewart's shop and asked for a janitor for her lamp instead of a generator. In her new garden coronations and lollipops flourished from the cuttings wheedled from my father's carnations and lupins and poppies.

"Put a bit of ding on them, mistress," she would say when my mother asked how she managed to grow geraniums so well. " Ding's the answer." She was too polite to say a rude word like dung to the schoolmaster's wife.

Once, after my mother had undergone surgery for an ulcerated duodenum, Mrs Miller paid her a visit to tell her how pleased she was that her 'illustrated stomach' was better.

The classic story about her tells of how she was ambling down the middle of the street near Tigh a' Chreagain, a gaunt house that used to stand alone on the rock of the seashore at the east end of the village. Tourists were beginning to use Lochcarron as a runway to the ferry at Strome and a big car came whizzing round the corner and nearly knocked Mrs Miller "into maternity" as she said later. The car stopped and a pompous ass said,

"My good woman, do you want to go to eternity?"

"Oh no. I'm just going to Dunkie's shop," she said and hopped in. Laughter was never very far away when Mrs Miller was about.

One morning, when my father was leaving to go to school, he called to my mother, "I'm off then. Cheerio, dear."

"Cheerio, dear," came Mrs Miller's voice from under the table.

When my Uncle Mac left after a prolonged visit, she saw him off at the door wiping her eyes on the dishcloth.

"Ah well," she said, "The best of friends must part."

Mrs Miller, otherwise known as Birdie, was incredibly thin – a tiny brown wren of a woman with stick-like legs, all bone and drooping lisle stockings, yet she marched about tirelessly. She seemed always to be in brown but that may be a trick of memory.

What I do remember is her horrible pixie hood – brilliant emerald green and holly-berry red. It was my first attempt at knitting 'a proper garment' after the 'useful' kettleholder made of triangulated squares. Knitting was a chore and that interminable strip was ripped back so many times I grew to loathe it. I finished it while in bed with the mumps and so hideous did I look in it that my mother immediately gave it to Mrs Miller, who collected rags.

She wore it for years. It made my neck ache every time I saw her wizened face framed in its gaudy glory.

After she retired from being a home help, Mrs Miller continued to visit and take tea with my mother. Her stories over the teacups were even more amazing than the little green men she reserved for me. I used to sit very quiet behind the sofa, hoping the grown-ups would not remember to send me out when the stories grew too blood-curdling.

One I remember reached its climax with these words;

"– and she hinged herself from the nail of the frying-pan so the Sahtan got her after all."

When I was in my twenties my parents moved from Lochcarron east to Maryburgh and soon afterwards so did Mrs Miller, widowed now, to stay with her married daughter. She came once in a while to call on my mother, always bringing a present of a dishcloth or a fancy tea-towel, relics of the pedlar's pack.

On her last visit she was very frail. She sat by the fire gazing at a picture my husband had painted of an old drove road in Skye. Nobody told her where it was but she knew.

"Many's the time Laochan and myself walked that track with the old cart," she said.

It was with sadness but no surprise that we heard shortly afterwards that she had died.

In her own words, "The best of friends must part."

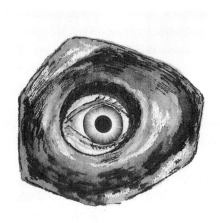

THE BRAHAN SEER

THE power of Coinneach Odhar, the Brahan Seer, lives on in the Highlands. We need him.

Every decade brings its own awareness of this 17th century prophet whose glimpses of other times and spaces, weird and incomprehensible in their time, have so often come to pass. Every now and then a fresh prophecy comes to the fore. Nobody knows whether it really emanated from Coinneach Odhar or whether it has arisen in the group consciousness or whether it is just a piece of mischief by some anonymous latter-day prophet

In the 1970s the Skye Gathering Hall in Portree was supposed to collapse cataclysmically when its doorstep became worn down to ground level. Somehow, and reports varied, a lame tailor and a girl in a red dress would be involved but nothing has happened except that the tailor has died and the doorstep has been replaced.

When the trunk road to Ullapool was under construction, rumour had it that Coinneach Odhar had prophesied a curse would fall on any-one who harmed the Brahan Rock. Local men refused to take part in blasting the road through that area and labour had to be recruited from elsewhere.

Many people thought it was sheer folly of Caledonian-MacBrayne to name their new ferry to Stornoway *The Isle of Lewis* since the Seer had mysteriously prophesied back in the 17th century that there would come a time when the Isle of Lewis would sink beneath the waves.

In the 1950s I was caught up in a Brahan Seeing myself. I was at school in Dingwall Academy and like the other West Coast pupils living in a hostel, a hotbed of gossip at the best of times. All of a sudden the word was out that the prophet had foretold that on a day when the sun turned black and noon became night an iron horse would be travelling through the Highlands with many children on its back. There would be a terrible disaster and none would be saved.

Fear ripped through the place like fire through heather. It was the end of term; we were due to travel home by train in a few days' time. And on that day there was to be a near-total eclipse of the sun, the first we had ever experienced. The day we longed for, marked the calendar for, now became a date of looming dread.

Some girls became hysterical; some persuaded their parents to come for them by car but most of us in those days were not so well-off. The grown-ups told us not to be so silly but by then the story had reached the local newspapers. How could we not believe it? We resigned ourselves to Fate.

Throughout all the speculation I refused flat to concede that there might be any possibility of truth in the prophecy. I pooh-poohed the whole thing as a piece of concocted sensationalism and I insisted we would be all right. It was sheer bravado. Inside I was as terrified as everybody else.

After prize-giving on the last day of term we trailed our suitcases and heavy hearts down to the station, certain like aristocrats in the tum-brils that it was our last journey. The train rattled west carrying a very subdued cargo of children for once.

At Achterneed a queer twilight began to grow eerie, menacing. It was true then. The eclipse had started, We sat tense and grim. Some of the First Years sobbed a little. Those of us who spoke had high-pitched voices and taut shrill laughter which did not last.

The shadow crept across the sun; the train crept across the summer landscape. Then just before Achanalt we came to the bridge over the River Brahan. Men were working on the track and the train slowed to walking pace, to a crawl, then stopped altogether, half on and half off the bridge.

"What's happening?" We whispered but nobody knew.

"Please God, I'll be good forever if only you'll let us get home safe," I said in my head.

The train began to inch across to the other side . . . slowly . . . slowly. Then we were over and away. gathering speed and very soon pulling in to Achnasheen. The Gairloch contingent exploded out of the compartments with hoots of relief and derision.

"We're safe now! *We're* all right! Ha! Ha! Ha!" We stared back stonily and pretended not to care.

There was nothing to do but endure. The train rocked and roared down Glencarron trying to make up for time lost at the bridge. We clutched each other and shivered and shook, certain that at any minute we would jump the rails and crash into the gully below.

The sun was returning; the gloom was lifting but our tension did not ease until the last of us tumbled on to the platform at Strathcarron and we stood in full sunshine, safe with our parents, the whole of the summer holidays stretching before us.

Ever since that day I have had a certain sympathy for Lady Seaforth. She had the Brahan Seer boiled in a barrel of tar.

THE SLUG BONUS

At the end of Fifth year a group of us took a holiday job in a canning factory in Dundee. We had led sheltered lives up until then but the girls' hostel had inured us to spartan conditions so our sleeping quarters in a boarded-up corner of the packing-shed did not come as a shock, nor did the bleak communal shower, nor the army camp-beds with their grey blankets and feather-leaking pillows.

But factory life was tough. From clocking-in to clocking-off we were static at a bench, flicking raspberries down rickety tin chutes into razor-edged cans. Crates packed with punnets stood beside each worker and the faster you emptied the punnets the more bonus you got.

It sounded easy but the reality was hard. Basic hourly rate was 2/11d and for that you had to empty several crates before you got any bonus. Even the best of us working flat out managed only a few extra pence daily but the Dundee women were experts. Small, tough and almost cube-shaped, their fingers were a blur. They made a phenomenal amount of bonus. They needed to; theirs was no holiday job. Punnets emptied, tins stacked up in pyramids around them faster than the belt could take them away. I had expected to be able to daydream, to let my brain wander while my hands worked but I soon found I became an automaton, part of the machine, all imaginative thought defeated. Boredom and backache through the weary hours, pressure sores on heels, and at the end of the day instead of sleep, all you saw behind your eyelids were torrents of raspberries. You couldn't talk as you worked, you could only yell. I saved my sanity by singing under my breath all day long.

My 'Hielan' accent' was a continual source of amusement to the Dundonians, I thought this was rich, considering how impenetrable I found theirs at first. One of the hands who shifted crates on a wee trolley loved to wheel up behind me and mutter in my ear,

"D'ye ken the Lobey Dosser?"

"What?"

"The Lobey Dosser. D'ye no ken the Lobey Dosser? "

"I know what a dosser is. Is it a tramp that sleeps in lobbies?"

Hoots of laughter. "Hey! She disnae ken the Lobey Dosser."

Away he'd go, only to return next day and start the whole silly joke over again. I could *not* discover what it meant. None of the other girls knew either. In the hostel we rarely saw newspapers. How could we guess the Lobey Dosser was a cartoon cowboy on a two-legged horse?

The afternoon tea break was the highlight of the day because trays of fresh baking arrived at the canteen – butteries, rowies, cream buns and vanilla slices. We queued eagerly at the counter.

"Gie's a perrisie," said the woman in front of me. Her white turban was level with my chin. I liked the look of the bright yellow bun scattered with sugar crystals she got, so –

"Can I have a perrisie too, please?" I asked politely.

Howls of laughter, wiping of eyes, slapping of backs greeted this.

'Oh! What now? What had I done this time?' Apparently the thing was properly called a Paris bun. How was I to know?

It was a great relief to me when I was given the job of emptying pulp cans. Each worker had a gallon tin beside her in which to put broken berries. Only whole and wholesome berries went into the cans; rubbish and husks and mouldy rasps were picked out and discarded on the bench and over-ripe berries went into the pulp cans to be sent for jam or Raspberry Ripple. I got my new job because I was tall. I could reach over and carry away gallon cans dripping pulp, one under each arm, to the hogsheads at the far end of the bench. Red and sticky from head to foot by the end of the day, I still thought this job was better than being stuck at the bench. I was on the move; I got fit. I became a character to the static workers. I was *"Morag, the toerag, the teuchter frae the North"*, a cartoon character myself, but it was better than anonymity. I played up to it and I still sang as I worked.

The hogsheads had personality too. Their names, MOG and GOB, were painted on their sides. Nobody could tell me why; nobody seemed to care. Years later I found the answer. I was driving along the Perth Road from my younger son's graduation when I passed an old farm sign and then another; *Mains o' Gray* and *Grange of Barry. MOG* and *GOB*, the farms that supplied the fruit!

DESPITE everything, some of us went back the following summer. We were in limbo between school and hostel life and the unknown; only the factory was familiar, grim as ever, the raspberry-stunned boredom just the same but it was freedom of a sort and we now had some spending money so on Saturdays we hit the town, frequented department stores, picture-houses and as we grew older and bolder, the dance-halls. We bought dresses and fancy underwear and high heels. We nicked bleach from the store to get rid of the tell-tale purple stains of raspberry juice. We experimented with cigarettes from the machine on the canteen wall. We eyed up the talent and were eyed in return.

I HAD my eighteenth birthday that July. I had always considered myself lucky to escape the bumps and all the humiliating tricks played on hapless birthday girls during term-time in the hostel. Now I threatened my best friend with hideous retribution if she told on me in the factory. She swore silence but at midnight on the 28th the inmates of the dorm rose up, lifted me bodily, mattress and all, carried me into the yard and dumped me in my baby-doll pyjamas right in the path the night-shift would take on their way to the canteen.

The hooter sounded; the girls vanished and I had no time to make a break for it. I pulled the grey blankets over my head and huddled in my cocoon praying that no one would pull the covers off. I could hear tramping feet and laughter and *Jings, Crivvens* voices straight from the Beano all around and above me. They said plenty but nobody touched. Nobody laid a finger on me.

I lay there an eternity until there was silence then I dared to peep out. An empty yard. Nothing but bare floodlit tarmac all the way to the road beyond the big gates. I picked up my bed and ran.

NEXT morning it was the speak of the factory. Everyone had a laugh at the big teuchter and I laughed too but this time I had the last laugh.

Reilly was the manager of the pea-canning side, a world of its own in another part of the factory, inhabited by old couthy men in cloth caps and young student types who clambered about yodelling over the clatter and cascade of machines that separated pods from vines and peas from pods and poured them into silver cans that chattered and squeaked and spiralled down from the can-lofts in the roof. One magic day Reilly had beckoned me to follow him away from the raspberries for ever, away into the world of green peas. He led me to a machine where I had to stand, usually in a puddle and a draught, but I didn't care, stacking lids into a column between three iron rods. That was all I had to do but for this my wage went up to 3/- an hour.

This was a man's world – far more interesting. I could look about, shout across the machine to the operator. I fed the lids; he made sure the cans did not stick in the chutes, that brine and peas were cascading accurately into the cans as they passed between us. They fell out of the lidder into large metal baskets then were whirled away to ovens to be steam-heated. Once, before my horrified eyes, one of the ovens blew back and the small man in a blue boiler-suit, who had been bantering with me a few moments before, was suddenly a scalded, twitching bundle on the sodden floor, stretchered out and never seen again.

REILLY kept an eye on me. He was a big, quiet Irishman with brown curly hair, a kindly fatherly man. I have always got on well with Irishmen. The weekend before my birthday the male students organised an outing to the Blairgowrie factory to a dance in the canning-loft.. I didn't enjoy it much. The boys had it all worked out and my pals were all paired off for a snog on the bus back. I didn't fancy the boy who fancied me and so I found myself at the end of my day of notoriety alone when they all went off to the pictures with their dates. Reilly spotted me at the 9pm tea-break, sitting alone with a fag and a book. He gave me a long look, said nothing much as usual, but a wee while later he crooked a finger at me from the door and offered me, a female student, work on the night-shift. Double pay! It was unheard of. My return to the dorm well after midnight that night was a triumph; the others were at first disbelieving and then very, very envious. They saw green peas in their sleep that night, not raspberries.

By then I had served my apprenticeship as a lidder and had been trained to operate the machine itself. I had a staff of office, a long pole to prod cans that stuck in the bends of the flumes, to keep them chattering. A large lever could halt the machine but that was a last resort. It was a disgrace if your machine jammed and the cascades of peas and jets of green brine had to be stopped.

Worst of all, if cans buckled and jammed in the machinery a wee man with a hammer and chisel and a fine line in withering scorn would arrive: *students were a' scunners, teuchters were toerags nae fit tae be in charge of grand auld machinery.* The red-faced operative had to stand and absorb his tirade till he had cleared the mess, then the line would start up, the workers who had had the chance to nip out the back door for a quick drag would give a wink and a grin in passing and all would be well again.

The peas arrived at the factory by the lorry-load on vines ripped straight from the fields. Once separated from the trash they danced down an endless stair on to a slow-moving belt on either side of which sat a picked bunch of Dundee women, with tin cans strapped to their belts. Their job was to pick out bad peas, stones, husks and,especially slugs, before the peas moved on to the canning machine. Nobody liked touching slugs so each slug carried a sixpence bonus. This was a fortune and the job was a coveted one. Students need not apply.

One day the word went round, *"No more slug bonus."* The factory was going on an economy drive. Lorries disgorged vines as usual; machines rattled and shook ; peas rolled along the white table and the Dundee wifies stood back and watched them go by. They unfolded their brawny arms every now and then to remove a stone but they let every slug go past to a briny grave in a can of peas. Slugs turn to froth when they encounter salt.

It was a whole morning before Quality Control got wise to all the new protein in the peas. Slug bonus was reinstated.

THE FACTORY was very proud of the *By Appointment* coat of arms printed on every label. One day my machine and the sorting-table were stopped and Reilly sent me to work with the slug bonus wifies. We were instructed to fill cases of very small cans with finger-picked peas, making sure they were all of top quality and similar size. Rumour had it that these were for the Queen. Poor Queen! Every single pea had been handled by one of her subjects, but at least she could be sure there were no slugs in the brine.

THE BEST day I ever had in the factory was once again thanks to Reilly. He enjoyed being mysterious; he never gave reasons. One morning my machine was not needed. I was kicking my heels when he came along with his beckoning finger. To my astonishment he led me out into sunshine across the waste lot behind the factory to a big metal tank lying among willowherb and thistles. He handed me a hammer and a chisel and asked me to chip flaking rust off the inside of the tank. I was delighted. I was out in the fresh air under a blue sky in my own private suntrap. Better still, the acoustic in the tank was simply wonderful. I sang and chipped and banged away blissfully all morning and well into the afternoon till, to my great disappointment, I was summoned back inside. The shop stewards had decided that was no work for a lassie and I was transgressing union rules. No more was said about it but I had had my day of freedom and now I had an enviable suntan into the bargain.

AFTER all this you would think I would never eat processed peas or fruit again but I do. I prefer them frozen though. The pick of the crop goes without delay to the freezers. It's as well to remember that.

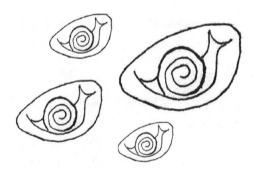

JOHNNIE COM

I used to watch Johnnie Com stumping round the corner of our street on his way home from the slaughterhouse, his dogs at his heels.

"Johnnie Com from Stormyhill
Never worked and never will."

He would quote this couplet against himself to make his cronies laugh in the pub, but it was not strictly true. Whenever there was any slaughtering to be done for the local butcher, Johnnie would go up to the little shed in the fields and do it. You could tell what he had been up to by the grisly load he carried home on a string – a trail of bloody offal and guts for his dogs. He would throw it on the ground at the side of the house and the long lean collies would wolf it down.

His house stood on the brow of Stormyhill; its gable turned to one of the best views of the Cuillins in Portree. Once it had been a snug little dwelling but all that remained was a roofless shell. Rumour had it that when his mother was alive the house had been one of the most homely and respectable in Portree, but once his family had all died Johnnie began to chop up the house for firewood. He began with the furniture and once that was done he stripped the walls of their pitch-pine lining. Then the floor went and finally the roof.

He continued to live within his three walls, entering by a collapsed portion of the back of the house. The windows and front door were blocked against prying eyes, but everybody knew he now lived in a lean-to built around the fireplace and composed mainly of wardrobes. It was a strange sight on a winter's evening to see a cheerful plume of smoke spiralling from the gaunt chimney-head of Johnnie's roofless ruin.

As long as he had his fire and his whisky Johnnie seemed to thrive. But fire and whisky were his downfall.

He used to frequent auction sales to buy up any bit of old worm-eaten furniture that was left at the end. He would pay a few shillings for them and pile them up around his house to burn when he needed them. When he had been slaughtering and had some money on him, he would have a good dram and fall asleep happily in front of a roaring fire of varnished wood.

At times like these, Johnnie would not have called the Queen his granny, but one night the fire was too big and the whisky too strong. He fell asleep with his wellingtons towards the blaze and the rubber melted and stuck to his feet.

When he woke up he was in a bad way, but for a good few days he never let on to a living soul.

He went for his food to the kitchen of the hotel and he stood with his cronies at the bar or at the end of the butcher's shop as usual and only when the pain got too much for him did he give in and put himself at the hands of the welfare state.

They took Johnnie into hospital; they cleaned him up and tucked him into a warm bed with loving care but he dwindled. His whisky drinking had played havoc with his liver and the shock of the burning and subsequent infection had drained his resources. With a roof over his head he was like a snail without a shell and without his lifestyle he had nothing to live for.

I went to see him in hospital. He had often had a crack with me over the fence as I worked to make a garden, and once he had asked me for two rhododendron bushes I was throwing out. He planted them beside his ruin where they languished under a decrepit buddleia and some straggling fir trees.

I wondered what to take him and decided on a bunch of flowers from my garden because I was sure no one else would do such a thing.

I made up a nosegay of the broom blossom he liked best and then went to the newsagent for an ounce of Black Twist. If they had banned his evil wee pipe perhaps he could chew it.

On impulse, I added a couple of sugar-mice for my wee boys to the purchase. There was just time for a hospital visit before I had to pick up my husband at the school.

My visit to Johnnie was a success. He was very surprised to see me, but pleased, as he sat up in bed looking strangely clean and sweet in his stripy pyjamas. We had a grand yarn about the old days when he crewed on the steam yachts for toffs sailing round the Hebrides.

Or when he drove a bus round the North End. One of the tourists asked him one day why there were so many rocks along the road at Score Bay.

"Well, it was like this," he said. "In the days of the Flood when Noah was sailing in the Ark, he got into a wee bit of trouble off the coast of Skye and he threw out a whole load of ballast!"

I could have listened to him for hours, but my family was waiting and I had to go. As I left I put a paper bag on his bed.

"Here's a wee present for you," I said and I hurried off before he could thank me.

When I reached the school I had to wait for my husband to finish cleaning up the art room. To while away the time I rummaged in my handbag. What was this? A small paper bag. I could not remember buying anything. To my horror it contained an ounce of Black Twist.

What had I given Johnnie Com?

For the life of me I could not remember. I broke out in a cold sweat. What else had I bought? Had I been to the chemist?

I sat there in sheer panic until it came to me – the two pink sugar mice!

When the art teacher came out to the car he found his wife a hysterical wreck, helpless and weeping with laughter. I could hardly tell him what I had done. I could hardly drive back to the hospital. I could hardly explain my mistake to the nurses.

I waited outside the ward, listening to the torrent of Gaelic and the shrieks of laughter as they handed over Johnnie's paper bag and retrieved mine.

Inside were the remains of two sugar mice nibbled down to their string tails.

STORMYHILL

It's gale force ten out there.
Foul weather wuthers round the gable-end.
Crows, coalsacks,
sweetie wrappers
scatter struggling
along the turmoil of the wind.
(How do birds breathe,
flying like battered kites?)
The street-lights whang.
Bare branches claw the air.
The door-lock mourns.

You need the leeside of a hill
to build your home up here.
And if you choose the hilltop for the view
then be prepared to sacrifice your peace.
You'll need deep roots
or heavy anchors,
sharp flukes like fingers clinging to the rock.
You must take care
to batten down your hatches,
to wrap up well and lean into the wind
to learn to love its threnody and song,
to greet your neighbours
with an understatement,
"It's breezy , right enough!"

THE WORMIT PATH

When Scott, my second son, left home, I found the empty nest unbearable. During the working week I was busy but I could not stay alone in the house at weekends and found any excuse to escape.

I had rented an attic flat for him in the centre of Dundee and had paid a retainer for a month before term started. While he was away at his summer job I had the keys for what became for a time my bolt-hole. The flat belonged to Martin, an artist acquaintance, who was seldom there. His work took him all over the country but he retained a room for himself and right of access, an arrangement that worked well enough for all of us throughout this transition time.

One weekend I arrived to find Martin in residence. This was no problem. He was busy and I amused myself around town or read and slept. We met at the teapot now and then and he told me his friend Kenny was coming to stay on Saturday night.

A hard man from Glasgow, he said, "So beware!"

Kenny had the Glaswegian patter but was a sensitive soul, proud of his Hebridean granny reputed to be a witch. I took to him right away.

Sunday morning arrived, bright and beautiful. I had the car so we decided to take a trip over the bridge to Fife. We climbed Norrie's Law and from the hill-fort viewed the Firth of Tay stretching far inland, then below us Fife's undulating patchwork of fields and woods and villages like Stevenson's "pleasant land of counterpane".

I picked berries and shared them; I found the well. I felt buoyant and happy and free up there on Norrie's Law.

It was too early to go back to Dundee so Martin suggested we drive down to Balmerino Abbey since Kenny and I had never been there.

There was little left of the abbey except notices telling where everything used to be; stone stumps in green grass, a crumbling chapter-house and an ancient chestnut propped on iron crutches. It is a place crippled by age and a bloody history.

Kenny and Martin found a seat in the sun and eventually I joined them, listening drowsily to their conversation. Somebody was making a bonfire nearby and sweet smoke drifted sleepily through the air. I felt relaxed and content just then. At peace.

Kenny talked about rottweilers with real affection; he talked of his ambition to be a cabinet-maker on his Granny's native island. He said he was the third son of a third son, not as powerful as a seventh son but formidable. I believed him.

After a bit we rambled away down a rose-scented lane to the shore. A track led to Wormit beside a beach of rocks and clean gravel. The tide was high and still flowing against the murky estuary current.

It all seemed pleasantly pastoral, a narrow tarred road skirting fields of grain, bird song and roses. But round the corner the mood changed completely.

Three large houses barred the way, straddling the path, two new holiday homes and a gaunt old sandstone farmhouse, cheek by jowl. A crude modern wall had been built out over the shore and infilled with imported earth and sparse new grass.

I stopped. I did not want to go on but Martin insisted. "They can't stop us. It's a public footpath. We have right of way."

But still I wanted to avoid the area so I clambered down to the shore and plowtered about examining pebbles.

Martin went ahead to reconnoitre, then Kenny joined him on the new lawn where they sat, rather defiantly I thought, deep in discussion.

I wandered back to where a huge round boulder higher than my head sat on the foreshore. I had remarked on it as soon as we turned the corner because it was so characterful and dominant. Now I walked round it sunwise, examining it closely – a glacial erratic, alien among the local sandstones, with veins of quartz running through pegmatite and strange ripple marks at its base as if it had been torn out of the matrix like an uprooted fungus. The marks seemed like a grin – not a pleasant one.

I put the flat of my palms on the rock to get the feel and sense of it. (Whenever I can I like to do that to stones and sculptures and the trunks of trees.) All of a sudden I began to feel very, very tired, very heavy. I left the rock and tottered over to a shingle bank below the road. Time slowed; the air grew thick and dark and the atmosphere pressed down on me, pressed me flat. I wanted to sleep but I couldn't. I lay there stupefied. I wanted to leave the place but I could not summon the energy.

I heard voices and laughter above me on the path and I thought they must think me crazy lying there like a beached whale but I could do nothing about it. I wished with all my heart that Martin or Kenny would come and rescue me. If I opened my eyes I could just see the tops of their heads talking, talking.

My feeling of foreboding grew and grew. Parallel to that, the left side of my brain kept telling me not to be so stupid. With a great effort I hauled myself up the sea-wall on to the road. I could bear it no longer; I had to escape. I walked with lead feet to the edge of the new grass. Beyond that I could not pass; it was as if I was up against a force-field. The men were still sitting blethering, Martin facing the road and Kenny the sea.

I was just going to call them to come away when two young men came running towards us from the farmhouse. They were alike, fair and lithe and laughing, dressed in white shirts and loose grey trousers. I waited because I did not want them to hear me and think I was silly. I did not see where they went; they did not pass me.

When they were gone I called urgently,

"Martin, could you come away, please? There's something wrong with this place."

To my relief, they did not ridicule; they did not question. They just got up and came at my bidding. Feeling daft but thankful, I turned and walked ahead of them along the road. I was shivering and felt very peculiar but as we turned the corner it was as if a great weight left me and the horror and nausea eased the further along the road we went.

A cargo boat was passing up the Tay and its wake began to reach the shore, swooshing up the shingle. Birds sang again and Kenny caught up with me.

"Have you noticed the sounds have begun again?" he said. "It's like going through a door."

"You felt that too?" was all I said and we made no further reference to it in front of Martin but fell back into our previous mood of happy wandering, back to Balmerino and the car.

But the tension made itself felt in my back. From feeling fit and free at the beginning of the walk I now had burning knot of pain at the base of my neck and by the time we reached Dundee it was like a red-hot knife in my spine. And I had a 200-mile drive ahead of me that evening!

While Martin made the tea, Kenny noticed my trouble and offered to give me a massage.

"I have healing hands," he said, "I'm like my granny." It was no idle boast. As he worked I confided in him that my back had been fine until that place on the shore

"It was very bad, wasn't it?" he said. "Don't think about it. Don't go back there. Look, your wee back's all tensed up just mentioning it."

He went on soothing and massaging the pain away till Martin called us to the table and after the meal I drove away home, stress-free.

I never saw Kenny again but a year or two later Martin visited me and we got talking about our walk on the Wormit Path. He had never heard this story, never been aware of my feelings that day because I had been afraid he would ridicule me. It was all news to him and he did not laugh, as I had thought he might; indeed, when I got to the bit about the two young men running down the road he just stared.

"There *were* no young men," he said. "Nobody on the road at all."

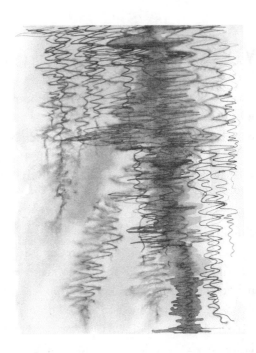

WILD IN THE COUNTRY

It was a Sunday in May. My boys were in their teens and my father had come to stay with us for a week or two. He loved coming back to the west, to see the sea, to talk Gaelic again and we enjoyed his company. Sundays were the only difficulty. To my father, a Strict Presbyterian, the Sabbath day was holy, a day for church, a day of rest. I can still see the look on his face when he caught me in the garden with a casual handful of weeds. Only works of necessity and mercy should be done on the Sabbath.

He knew fine we were backsliders, that Harry and the boys did not go to church but he said nothing. I did my best to keep everybody happy, forbade loud music and television while Grandpa was about, gave him his meat and two veg. at lunchtime and served dinner to the rest of us when he went to evening church. It was a strain but I managed.

Anyway, his lunch was over and he had gone up to his room; the others had only recently had breakfast. All of a sudden I had a bit of time to myself.

I walked straight out the door and away, off round the bay just the way I was. Free.

Above the footpath by the shore bracken fiddle-heads were pushing up through a mist of bluebells and old brown stalks. A cuckoo was calling in the hazel wood. Sabbath peace should have been hanging over moor and sea but instead, a helicopter was hovering over the bay, battering the water with its downdraught. The rescue services were practising putting men in and out of rubber boats.

Entertained by this, I loped along, stretching my legs, glad of the solitude, but just when I thought I had the track to myself, up popped a couple of tourists.

"Are you local?"

"Yes." I expected to be asked the name of some landmark or other.

"Oh good! There's a dog along there worrying a sheep and a lamb. You'll know what to do about it. "

Off they went at a rate of knots.

Round the corner was a young collie dog. It had separated a lamb from its mother and was standing over it among the rocks right down at the edge of the sea. The sheep was on the steep slope above the track bleating piteously and the tide was coming in.

What on earth was I going to do about this? I sent up a swift prayer that the dog would come if I whistled. It did! It left the lamb and came bounding towards me, a silly grin on its face. Next prayer was, "Oh please let it have a collar so that I can grab it." That prayer was answered too.

So there we were. I now had the dog but – wait a minute – I needed a leash. I was dressed in a summer frock and sandals: no belt, no tights, no pockets. It was a warm day and I had walked out of the house without even a cardigan. I looked around for a bit of rope or string. No fences, no flotsam, nothing on the tideline of the steep and rocky shore. I was about a mile in either direction from any habitation and there was not another soul in sight.

The dog was bounding and straining and already I could feel a hot red ache in my shoulder. Then I had my brainwave. Somehow, without letting go of the dog, I undid my bra and, with a bit of wriggling, slid it out of the armhole of my dress. I tied it to the dog's collar and off we went towards Torvaig, to the crofts round the headland. I had to leave the sheep and I worried about the lamb but at least I now had the dog captive and I could turn it in to Andy, the shepherd. I knew the township had been having trouble with sheep-worrying and here was the culprit bang to rights.

The dog was young and eager and bounded along happily beside me. Every now and then I could hear my bra rip and I hoped against hope that the material would hold till we got to civilisation.

Past the aspen grove, up the hill where the orchids grow, in and out amongst the tumbled scree to the old march dyke. There, coming down the path from the hilltop, was John the Caley and his spaniel on their daily constitutional.

"Hallo! " I yelled. "The very man I want to see. I need your help. There's a lamb and a sheep..."

"Aye," he said dryly. "I know. I saw it all from the top of the hill. You did well."

I burst out laughing. Saw it all, did he? O - kay!

"Well, if you see to the lamb, I'll take the dog up to Torvaig," I said.

Away we went, straight up the hill through bracken and bluebells, the dog tugging me on and up the slippery, soft slope faster than my sandals wanted to go.

I was hot, scruffy mess by the time we reached the top. Perched on a hillock, black against the skyline were a man and a woman watching a cow and a very new calf. They were so intent they never noticed me and I did not want them to. I had to keep the dog out of sight in case the cow took fright, so I doubled up and skulked along a dip in the ground using cover like a commando along under the horizon, keeping the dog low to the ground till I could get near enough to attract their attention. They were trying to encourage the young heifer to suckle her first calf and she was being a bit flighty about it.

When they heard my story about the dog and the bra and John the Caley they laughed so much they nearly fell off their hillock. The lady phoned Andy and brought me a welcome drink of barley water. Sunday or no Sunday, Andy came round at the toot, very grateful indeed. But he wouldn't take the dog from me until they had got him some baling twine to replace my hot, grubby bra.

They wanted to hear my story all over again.

"You'll have to send a bill to the township clerk for a new bra," they said, "So that we can have a good laugh again at the AGM."

"Of course not! I don't want payment."

"Oh! But you must."

That was it. We all went our separate ways: Andy impounded the dog, the cow took to her calf and I walked away down the hill back to the town with the ruins of the bra still clutched in my hand. I was back among the pavements before I realised I should have asked for a bag to put it in. There I was walking out of the wood, scratched and dishevelled, with my underwear in my hand.

And on the Sabbath too!

All this time the helicopter had been winching little men in and out of wee rubber boats, roaring up and down the bay. And who should be sitting on the bench at the top of Fire Station Brae watching it all with obvious enjoyment but my father!

There was nothing for it but to sit down beside him and make a clean breast of the whole affair.

Like all the rest of them he had a good laugh and like all the rest of them he told me I had done well.

It was, after all, a work of necessity and mercy.

That wasn't the end of it either. Just before Christmas I received a cheque for £25 with the grateful thanks of the Torvaig Grazings Committee. Enough to buy several bras.

THE WAYFARER

"Fancy a sail with me tomorrow?"
"I thought you would never ask!"

I had been waiting all summer for Jim to invite me to crew for him. It was now the first of October and I should have been helping with Harvest Thanksgiving but this was too good a chance to miss. Jim's own yacht needed repairs so he had borrowed the school's *Wayfarer*, which was on our friend Rob's mooring.

We hauled it in and bailed it out. I was used to this. I had grown up with wooden clinker-built boats that always took on a bit of water. Jim's own boat had a cabin and a bilge pump.

This *Wayfarer* felt flimsy and plastic by comparison but we adjusted to it and once past Vriskaig Point we caught the breeze and scudded along.

The morning mist was rising, breaking into tatters and folds around the great basalt crags of Beinn Tianavaig and the sun was highlighting our sails with a dazzling contre-jour effect. Pinnacles and buttresses loomed black against the brilliance. Rafts of razorbills and guillemots dived at our approach, then surfaced beyond us again and again.

Soon we were out past the caves at Tom Head. Raasay Sound opened up before us and we danced along with the breeze in our backs. And then we saw the sea eagle! There it was, hanging so motionless on the rising air that it seemed to have abolished gravity. We saw its white tail; we saw the great span of its wings. We stared, thrilled, till the vast bird was just a dot in the sky.

How quickly things change! The crew had been neglecting to bail; the floorboards were deep in water. Jim decided we had gone far enough so we went about and all of a sudden we were in deep trouble. Bailing became an imperative, half a bucketful at a time. I bent and scooped and flung, bent and scooped and flung to empty the bilges. Meantime Jim was wrestling with a boat that would not respond now to the tiller.

The wind had freshened dramatically. Gone was the friendly sea and instead blue-black waves, white-topped by successive squalls came at us across the bay. We had no time to be frightened or to speak to each other. I bailed for our lives, one hand for the bucket, the other for the jib-sheet. When a squall struck we had to let the sails flap or the boat threatened to capsize. Sometimes the wet rope stuck in the cleat and I had to drop the bucket and use both hands to jerk it free.

I begged Jim to shorten sail. The halliards kept jamming and he tore the skin off his fingers. It was the only time he swore! We both kept cool and worked as a team without argument. We knew each other's body language because we regularly played and sang in a band. I think that saved our lives.

By reefing the sail, keeping her well up into the wind and letting everything go the minute a squall approached, we managed to tack back into the lee of Beinn Tianavaig. All our attention was concentrated on the sails, the ropes, the bailing, but now and again through sharpened senses and heightened perception I'd catch a glimpse of something glorious – a cloud of gannets diving for mackerel beyond Beal Point, sun on the pinnacles above Scarf Caves, rocks bristling with cormorants.

Water sloshed to and fro, making the boat sluggish to steer. We were bruised and wet but oblivious to discomfort. Adrenalin was pumping; survival was all. No time to talk except to say, "Steady about" or "Use the cleat now."

The very worst moment came when a squall struck and I didn't let fly the jib soon enough. The rope stuck in the cleat. Jim needed both hands for tiller and mainsail sheets. We heeled right over. Water outside nearly met the water inside as the gunwale lipped the waves inches from my horrified eyes. I stood up and yanked at the jibsheet. The rope jerked loose, the sails flapped free, the boat stood upright and the squall passed.

"If we get to Camas Bàn I'll be so thankful, I'll be good forever," I prayed, but we were making so little headway on every tack, the beach at Camas Bàn seemed an impossible distance away.

I began to calculate our chances. "If this boat capsizes or even sinks, what can I do?" I knew I could swim a mile in the pool; I had done life-saving. Could I save myself? Could I save Jim too? Would anyone notice our distress in time? There was nobody about on land or sea so early on a Sunday morning. I faced death and I was too busy be afraid of it.

We came in close to Sgor on the port tack. Could we ground the boat there and try to make for the shore? A desperate idea. The high tide was covering some very inhospitable reefs.

Jim thought that if he worked the next tack right we might just make the beach at Camas Bàn, so we went about and gradually, miraculously, the fickle weather eased and it became plain sailing again. Soon I could use both hands for bailing; soon Jim at the helm was in control again and we tacked into Camas Bàn in pleasant autumn sunshine.

We pumped the beastly boat dry, left it at anchor, splashed ashore and flung ourselves on the beautiful safe grass, euphoric with relief, but we could not stop long because the tide was ebbing fast and the boat was filling up again.

Two longish tacks took us round Vriskaig and within sight of home but then we heard an ominous swishing sound.

"We're aground!" I raised the centreboard a little. (I had done this before in my childhood in Lochcarron.)

"We'll capsize!" Jim yelled.

"Not if you let down the sails. We'll have to row."

Jim got out the oars and I began to punt with the spare only to find the water was ankle-deep! So I stepped overboard.

"Come on!" I said. "I'm fed up with this boat."

We tidied the boat, hove out the anchor and abandoned ship, then giggling like idiots we waded the mile or so through the sea to our moorings carrying the oars and, for some reason, Jim's wellies.

Sunlight glinted and sparkled; the water was warm and walking was easy on firm sand. Exhilarated, gloriously, beautifully alive and happy we squelched, dripping, up to Rob's back door.

Later when the boat was retrieved, Rob discovered a nine-inch, T-shaped tear in the fibreglass hull, probably made by flotsam in the equinoctial gales the previous week. As teachers, we could only be thankful that we had found the fault and not the kids in the school sailing club.

PINK PAINT

My son's graduation day was one of the worst days of my life. It should have been a high spot, a goal achieved in a family deeply committed to education but it was not. In an *annus horribilis* it was *dies horribilissima*.

My husband had walked out the year before – his way of solving our domestic problems. It was a lean year for all of us. My salary as a teacher went to pay off debts and support my two sons in Art College. We managed, just. I was struggling in the dark all that year, keeping things afloat, occasionally plumbing the depths but always bobbing up again. By the time the summer brought the prospect of graduation I was feeling we were over the worst. I was very proud to receive the invitation to attend the ceremony in Glasgow.

At school it had not been easy either. My school was a rural two-teacher primary in a west-coast beauty spot.

Idyllic? Sometimes. It was hard, rewarding work, teaching and running the school and on the whole the children were delightful but that year there were two boys in P6 and P7 who were ruining the place for all the others, myself included. The old analogy of the rotten apples spoiling the barrel kept coming to mind all that year. They bullied, they cheeked, they were disruptive but not all the time and compared to kids in my previous city school they were pussycats. So I made the best of it.

Unfortunately, the graduation ceremony was to be on the day our school closed for the summer holidays, not a day I would ever think of being absent had it not been such a special one for me. It had been my dream to go to art college myself but my father would not hear of it.

"Art is all very well but it's a waste of a good brain. Go to university and learn something useful," had been his diktat.

I got my own back; I married an artist and had two sons with far more artistic talent than either of us. It was my dearest wish now to see them through art college, since that is where they had chosen to go.

So here we were, the goal achieved. I made arrangements for class cover, left the school to my capable assistant and off I went to Glasgow.

Not without trepidation. My husband (ex) would be there. He too was a proud parent not to be denied the moment of glory.

To give him his due he tried very hard. He had booked lunch for us all at a good restaurant and had taken extra care with the ordering but the day went wrong right from the start.

We were all uncomfortable, trying too hard to be normal and pleasant. Ross was depressed, felt he should have done better, wanted away with his friends.

"I won't see them again after today."

Parents were just a drag. I remembered my own graduation day and how my friend and I had gone out of our way to please our proud parents all day long because we felt we owed it to them.

And it rained. Sullen Glasgow rain.

We grew more miserable and stressed as the day wore on. It took longer to get through the traffic than expected and we reached the hall only just in time.

Ross disappeared in a flutter of gowns to get ready and we took our places in the gallery not knowing now what to say to each other.

The ceremony was boring. All I remember of it was one of the grandees telling the students they were the *crème de la crème* but that they had chosen the hardest path and very few of them would ever succeed in art.

Just what we needed to hear!

Afterwards we were supposed to go for a strawberry tea in the Union. It meant more trailing through wet streets, queuing on stairs, waiting for very indifferent cups of tea and cardboard-and-jelly tarts; it was the very last straw.

Long before this, we should have admitted we were a dysfunctional family and gone our separate ways. As we sat in our wet coats staring at the tea, husband began raking up old grievances; graduate son said, "That's it! I'm off!"

Wife, to her horror, burst into tears – huge deep sobs, howls of grief.

There, among all the middle-class strawberry tarts of Glasgow I lost control. The year's sorrows reared up and swamped me. I ran for cover in the lavatory, thinking I could mop up and return but I was aghast to discover I couldn't.

Something had broken inside me and I could not stop. I cried, wept, snorted and gurgled, awash with tears. I was mortified but helpless to stop crying. I needed air; I needed escape. Head down, I shoved my way upstairs past the still-descending, strawberry-searching masses, and ran away.

It was a relief to find outside that Glasgow was weeping too. The rain had turned into a deluge. Gutters were spouting, drains were overwhelmed. Umbrellas jostled; people ran. Everyone had a drip to their nose, everyone had wet faces. I was suddenly inconspicuous.

I ran, sobbing, from street to street with no idea where I was going. For a while I didn't care. I recall noticing a downpipe sending out a jet of water from a hole in its side and remembering in spite of myself a science lesson from school about water pressure. There were waterspouts everywhere in Glasgow that afternoon and not a hope of a rainbow.

At last I came to my senses a little. I was lost but I had an address. I was to stay with people I knew slightly, south of the river. There was no telling where south lay from that leaden sky and no chance at all of flagging a taxi but then I had an idea. Still in tears, still sobbing, I searched for a station where I knew there would be a taxi-rank and at last I found one and collapsed into the sanctuary of a black cab. On a news stand nearby I noticed that Lord MacLeod of Fiunary, George MacLeod of Iona, had died. One more bleak thing.

The taxi-driver noted my sobs but said nothing. He left me alone and I continued to cry all the way to the river and into the flat. I cried to myself for several hours; I cried myself into exhaustion. I have never known anything like it.

My friends were out until late evening so I had nothing to do but get over it and eventually I had no more tears. When they came home I was in a strange heightened state, a thin place, that's what George MacLeod would have called it. I got sympathy and comfort and I slept and next morning I repaid their hospitality by driving Bill across Glasgow with a fridge for his mother.

I am not used to town driving so by the time we came back I was exhausted again. I turned down the offer of a pub lunch and made straight for bed. I longed to be horizontal. The last thing I remember as my head hit the pillow was the clock on the wall saying ten past one.

I went straight to sleep, or so it seemed, but a few minutes later I sat bolt upright again, staring at the clock.

"HARRIET! PINK PAINT!"

I said it out loud, a clear picture in my mind of my assistant teacher standing in the back lobby of the school holding a plastic bottle of pink poster paint.

It was a dream. I shook my head and fell back into oblivion, slept all afternoon and by next morning was well enough to drive myself back on the long road home.

The summer diaspora had begun. Harriet was off to France. I was very surprised to get a letter from her on the following Monday, written on the ferry to Roscoff. She wanted to clear her mind so that she could enjoy her holiday. It seemed that the last day of term had not gone well despite my careful plans. The two bullies had incited their classmates to strike but the teachers had controlled the situation well and the rest of the morning had passed peacefully.

After lunch the school car came and took the bullies away, to everyone's relief, but the children, who had to wait for the school car's second trip, came running.

"Come and see, miss. Come and see what Angus and Billy have done!

They led her out to the old coalshed. The rough stone walls had been splattered and sprayed with a random graffiti of paint.

Harriet went into the back lobby where the art cupboard was. She stood there, bursting with frustration and fury because the culprits had cocked their final snook and escaped. They were finished with primary school.

Her anger must have transmitted itself to me because at that very time I had reared up in bed in Glasgow exclaiming, "Harriet! Pink Paint!"

She made no mention of the colour of the paint in her letter but I had an eerie feeling I knew what it would be. I had to go and make sure, so I drove out to school, half-hoping the graffiti would be green.

But there, all over the *inside* of the coalshed (I said they were pussycats), were squirts and trails and dribbles of the exact shade of pastel magenta I had visualised in Glasgow.

A JERSEY FOR MY SON

The knitting grows
under my fingers,
two plain, two purl
and pass the slip-stitch over.
A jersey for my son
to keep him warm next winter
far away.

I see a hair
caught in a mesh of stitches,
one of my long fair hairs.
I want to leave it,
part of me
close to his chest
each time he wears the wool.
But no.
I snap the brittle tendril,
set him free
to live and love.
He owes me nothing more.
I cannot keep him tethered to my heart.

I knew a woman once
netted a man
for whom she laid long lures.
As soon as he was hers
she took the sweater
that her rival knitted,
ravelled out the stitches

then rolled the wool in skeins,
washed and reknitted it
to her own pattern.
Thus she proclaimed
she owned him.

Lovers and brothers,
husbands, sons,
we long to clothe them,
save them, own them
but a wise woman
will not weave her love
into hair-shirts
to make their lives
a penance.

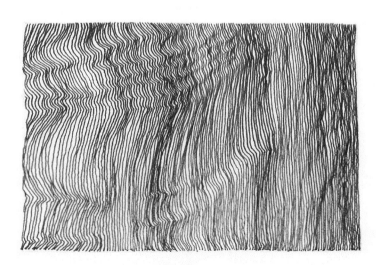

THE ZUNI FETISH

I WENT with Martin, my son's landlord, one day to visit a traveller who lived near Dundee. The ceilidh went on from two in the afternoon until midnight with songs and stories and food and drink in abundance. Sometime during the afternoon I needed to stretch my back, so, listening to the crack all the while, I washed the piles of dirty dishes that cluttered the kitchen, relics of a past ceilidh.

When the traveller's wife, an American woman, came home she was pleased with this and became very friendly, inviting us to stay the night. And so the ceilidh went on and we began to use up all the dishes and glasses all over again.

At one point in the evening she disappeared into her room and came back with some thing in her hand, which she gave to me. When I opened my palm there was a little stone beast, white with a pointed nose, prick ears and a pointed tail. It had a tiny turquoise dagger strapped to its back.

"It's for you," she said. "I want you to have it."

"Oh!" I cried, delighted. "For me? What is it?"

"I don't know. I call it the badger."

"It's more like a fox or a wolf. Is it really for me? Oh! Thank you very much. It's beautiful."

"You may not be so pleased with it yet," she said.

Strange words to give with a gift! They cast a chill on my pleasure but I let the moment pass. I held the wee beast in my hand till it turned warm and then I put it away in a safe pocket.

The men watched this exchange. Not to be outdone, the traveller leaped up.

"I have something for you," he said to my friend and gave him a Native American medicine bag from the mantelpiece. Martin laughed and put it in his pocket too.

We stayed the night and after a pleasant breakfast we left and that was that – or so I thought.

I went home but no sooner had I arrived than my life seemed to come apart around me. Out of the blue a vendetta started against me at work. It turned into a witch-hunt. From March till November of that year I was struggling to clear my name, to save my reputation and my job.

When eventually I won through, my health, which had been already precarious, began to crack under the strain and in due course this led to my having to give up my career permanently. Nothing was ever the same again.

I had forgotten the wee stone creature but one day I found it in its safe pocket and I put it on display on my shelf. One night at the height of my troubles I was sitting at home alone, too sick at heart to light the fire or make the tea. I found my gaze focussed on the ornament and the American woman's words came back to me with full force. It seemed to me that I had not had a moment's luck since she had given me her gift.

Now, I am a Ross-shire woman. My ancestors are all Ross-shire people right back through the generations and the word that came to me then was the buisneach! Scratch a Ross-shire person, be they ever so religious, or, in this day and age computer-sophisticated, and you will still find a knowledge of the buisneach – the curse, the bad wish, the evil eye. And things can be made to carry the buisneach as well as words or thoughts, or so it is believed.

The wee white carving sat on the shelf while reason struggled with superstition across the room. I had to get rid of it just in case. Just in case there was anything in the old belief. I liked the beastie; I wanted it but I could no longer keep it. Why on earth had the American woman uttered those dubious words?

What was I to do? I could not pass it on as she had, just in case it carried the buisneach. I could not ill-wish anyone, not even those who were making my life a misery, though I was sorely tempted. I could not throw it away because it was too fine an artefact. I could not break it. I thought of all these things and rejected them.

And then I had an idea. I thought of a name, let's say it was John Maxwell. I thought of a number, 41, an address, Coombe Road. I wrapped the creature in some tissue, put it in a jiffy bag and sent it to my random address in Perth where I knew there was a big sorting-office and a dead letter centre.

I had a long road and a hard struggle before I came through the next months and years of darkness and fear and ill-health out into the light again but gradually I recovered and a new life began to take shape.

A year or so after all this, I had a visit from the friend who had been with me at the traveller's house and, as the evening grew late round my fireside, the stories grew eerier as they do and I found myself telling him the tale of the wee stone beast and what I had done.

He looked at me sideways and said that he had never felt right about the gift he had got that day either. Things had taken a turn for the worse with him too and he had at last thrown his gift away and felt the better of it.

Neither of us could quite bring ourselves to believe fully that any evil had been intended. How could there be? It had been such a pleasant friendly encounter. And yet. And yet. It was all very strange.

A year or two after that I got the chance to go to California to stay with a friend. One day we visited a trading post in Davenport where there was a very chic, very expensive shop selling ethnic souvenirs. There in a glass case I came face to face with my wee stone beast. There it was, pointed at both ends, little prick ears, turquoise dagger strapped to its back with a piece of raffia. My heart gave a thump. It was a Zuni fetish, a white wolf and there were many other creature carvings orientated to the different poles of the earth, each with its own power.

In the display too were books by Frank Hamilton Cushing who had studied the Pueblo Indians, their culture and their customs before the building of the railways had destroyed their natural way of life.

I discovered that the Pueblo Indians have created an industry of making fetishes for the tourist trade. Those in the glass case cost about $50. I had sent fifty dollars worth of fetish to the dead-letter centre in Perth! I laughed to myself but somehow the memory of the fetish, now revived in California, would not let me go. It stayed in my mind. I now knew that the white wolf was one of the most favoured of all the fetishes and as far as I could tell it held no intrinsic tendency to anything but good luck. So why had the American woman said what she had said? Why had she tainted her gift?

I went home without a fetish but with a great deal more knowledge about them. And knowledge casts out fear. I now had a story to tell and each telling honed it and polished it just as the Pueblo craftsman had done with his white wolf.

Just recently I went back to California, back to Davenport. The trading-post was the same, very busy for Thanksgiving weekend. Compulsion drew me to the glass case. The Zuni fetishes were still there. A different display, of course, but there they were. I had no intention of buying one, though over the years my feeling of loss for the one I had sent had grown – a feeling of loss and yet a constant feeling that what I had done had been right. I could not afford fifty dollars for a whim and a bauble but I wanted to hold the wee beast in my hand again just for a moment.

There were two white fetishes, one with prick ears and a pointed tail, the other more rounded, more kindly. Both had bright turquoise daggers strapped to their backs. I gave my purchases to the girl behind the counter and asked if I could see the Zuni fetishes. She handed me the rounded one, the bear, first. As my hand closed over it I could almost feel the click as the story came full-circle.

"How much is it?" My voice seemed to come from far away.

"This one? This one is fourteen dollars."

I could afford it. It was for me. I had no feeling about the other one at all. It seemed to fade and grow dull as it lay on the counter *and* it was a good deal more expensive.

The shop was crowded but at our desk there was a lull so the two, sophisticated, Californian attendants wrapped my purchases together. I stood quiet and happy watching them.

"Have you a particular animal fetish?" said one girl. "I see you wear a cat pin in your coat."

"Oh no." I said, taken by surprise, "But there is a story behind my purchase of the bear."

They stood expectantly, those busy, glossy girls and I realised with a sinking heart that the story was going to find a way out. I tried to evade it. It was too long and complicated; I was too tired; we had no time, but to my amazement I found that they were extracting the tale from me, bit by bit, questioning me eagerly. It was as if we were in a place of our own. Nobody came near us all the time we were talking.

"And what did you do?"

"How did you get rid of it?"

"What happened then?"

There was no escape. I had to tell them the story from beginning to end and as I did so I saw astonishment in their eyes, astonishment and growing respect.

I put the new fetish in its box in a safe pocket just as I had done before and just as before, I forgot about it for a week or two after I got back. And then I could not find it. I thought it had gone. I thought I was not meant to have it after all. Until one day it turned up in the safe pocket of the coat I had not worn since coming home.

Now the little white bear sits on my mantelpiece, kindly and benign, its turquoise dagger strapped to its back.

But what happens now remains to be seen.

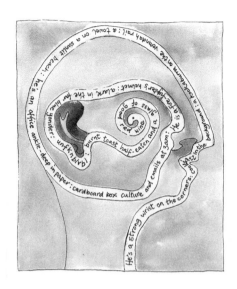

MORE ABOUT THE FETISH

YEARS passed. Martin disappeared; Scott graduated, got married and left Dundee. My connection with the town was at an end.

It looked as if the Zuni fetish story had reached an inconclusive end too until one day I got a phone call to say that Laura, the American woman, now divorced from the traveller, was to hold a story-telling session in a nearby church hall. Here was my chance to question her. Would I take it?

"Go on," said a friend, who knew the story. "You've got to find out why she gave you the fetish."

So I drove to the next town, feeling very strongly that I must let events take their own course. I would force no issues, let the story create itself.

The church hall was uncomfortable, all wrong for story-telling. Neon strip-lights glared; electric fires on the walls clunked on and off every few minutes but Laura had tried hard to create some intimacy; chairs were arranged round an oriental rug and a trolley of puppets and musical instruments stood by her place. A tea-urn was bubbling in the kitchen.

Several locals recognised and welcomed me but Laura did not. She rose, shook my hand, introduced herself and the man who is now her partner, then promptly forgot my name, which is the sort of thing I do myself and, to tell the truth, had I met her in the street I would not have known her either. She looked thin and stretched and her eyes stared in a way that reminded me of my mother, who had thyroid trouble.

It was all a bit stiff and stilted. I sat quiet and watched and listened. Laura told formal folk tales quite well, sang a ballad very well, used puppets but never really let herself go. She told riddles, far too many riddles. I realised her act was geared towards school visits. Riddles are like jokes, snappy things for kids with a short attention span. Embarrassingly, because there were prizes, I kept guessing the answers.

All the while I was wondering whether I would say anything about the fetish or not. It was my own private suspense and it kept the evening interesting for me. I felt pretty sure my time would come and it did.

A local man, Domhnall Angie, was supporting her programme, no mean seannachie himself. He told a few tales then said there was talent in the audience; he wanted to share the floor with us and make a proper ceilidh of it.

 Laura rather reluctantly invited a woman from Lochalsh to sing, then immediately took back the limelight with more riddles, but DA was keeping an eye on me; he knew my capabilities. He launched into an anecdote about a witchcraft trial in Harris someone suspected of laying a curse on a cow. And there it was at last my opening.

"Would you call that the buisneach?" I said to him.

"Buisneach or not, that's what happened. What I told you is true."

"Well, I have a true story too with a bit of the buisneach in it and I will tell it to you after we have our cup of tea."

Laura looked at me with her cold, staring eyes and said nothing. She got up and went to the kitchen where the churchwarden was seeing to the urn.

"Well, before the tea, give us a Gaelic song," said Domhnall Angie so I sang *Mìle Marbhaisg,* a lively waulking song.

The contingent from the Gaelic College sat up and took notice. Laura came back, took up her bodhran and added a neat backing to my singing. Things livened up; the ice was broken at last.

Tea and cake added to the warmth and the crack and we had to be called to reluctant order so that the session could start again.

More riddles! But then Domhnall Angie said to me, "Now, let's hear your story."

I began by saying: "I don't know how this is going to turn out." Not something a storyteller should admit, but it was the truth. The story was in the making. We *were* the story, here and now.

I went on.

"A number of years ago, quite a number of years ago, I visited a friend on the East Coast and he suggested we visit a storyteller friend of his one day . . . "

I took pains to paint a vivid picture of the warmth and welcome we had received, to praise the hospitality, the songs and the stories. For the first time all evening I saw Laura's face light up. I had no sense yet that she was relating the story to herself but I could see I was bringing good memories back to mind.

Well, I told the story from then on much as I have told it to you, allowing that the medium changes the message. I had their full attention. I could feel their intensity. When I said I had sent the fetish to Perth I saw Laura's man catch her eye. Did they live there now? Did he live there then? I don't know.

When I reached my second visit to Davenport I produced the little bear from my pocket and held it on my palm as I told them about the glossy girls coaxing the story out of me.

"I answered all their questions," I said, "Except the one question at the heart of the story.

"Why did the American woman say what she said? Without that there would be no story. Any time I have told this tale people are always left asking, 'why did the American woman say what she said'?"

And I stopped there.

There was a sigh and dead silence. I was looking at Laura who had been intent on my telling the whole way through.

"Was that me?" She said at last. "Did I say that?

I nodded.

"Something like that."

"I'm very sorry if I put you through all that."

"I don't believe you did, but once the idea had got into my head it had power and I had to do something about it."

Everyone agreed with this, especially the church elder.

"I got three of those fetishes," she said, "And I had to bury one of them."

DA broke in at this point with one of his anecdotes about someone stirring the ground and nothing growing thereafter but as soon as he was done I turned back to Laura.

"Do you think you could tell us, if it's not too private, why you had doubts about the fetishes?"

She avoided answering directly.

"You obviously know more about them now than I do. I remember you now. We were given three fetishes by Pueblo Indians who visited us just before you did with a Navajo called Moonflower who left a medicine bag. (This was the gift passed on to Martin who had in his turn dumped it because it felt uncanny. I kept quiet about this.)

"The fetishes were for me and my two children," Laura went on, "but I buried one of them under a tree. I had to."

Her voice began to sound strained.

DA, hearing the crack in her voice and sensing the weight that had seemed to descend on us all, said in his interrupting way, "Now lassie, I think you should sing us *The Lord of the Dance* "

Instantly the mood lightened. Laura got out her tambourine and danced and sang and so the evening ended.

Almost.

Before I left Laura came up to me to ask if she could hold my white bear fetish in her hand.

"I have to tell you the bear is my inner animal in Native American belief."

I laughed. "The first puppet you placed on the rug this evening was a lion, my star sign. I hope you did not mind me doing this to you."

"No. Not at all. I remember you now." She told me the traveller was well and that they still met and toured occasionally south of the border. We hugged and said goodbye and so my story ends.

But there is still mystery at the heart of it.

Why did she have to bury the second Zuni fetish and what became of the first one?

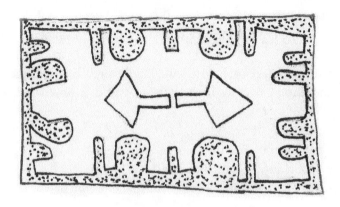

YO

I WENT to Tel Aviv in 1992 to stay with a friend called Ariela. We had met at the Skye Folk Festival. Both teachers, both singers, we found we had a lot in common. One day we took a bus up to Acco, the old Crusader port of Acre in the far north-west, almost on the Lebanon border.

We had a good time sight-seeing but by late afternoon we were weary and hot and footsore and when we got to the bus station I collapsed with such a loud sigh of relief that a bunch of Arab lads burst into giggles and somebody asked if I was all right.

"Yes," I said. "Just tired".

And then I noticed I was sitting beside a piece of unattended luggage! At that time security in Israel was far tighter than anything we had yet experienced in mainland Britain

"Oh! Perhaps not." I said, looking at the bag.

"What are you going to do?" They asked.

"Nothing. If it goes off I won't know anything about it and I'm too tired to care."

Everybody laughed a bit nervously and Ariela casually distanced herself and began to chat up an elderly Japanese archaeologist in a white sun hat.

I stared into space and rested thankfully until a very large Palestinian came striding over the backs of the seats and sat down beside me. A giant.

"It's your bag is it?" I said.

"Yes. Were you worried?"

"Och. Not really. Too tired to care."

He laughed and we got talking - the usual question first. Where I was from?

I told him I lived on the Isle of Skye in Scotland.

"Ah! Scotland!" he said. "I have a friend in Scotland. He is a shepherd."

"Oh yes?" Vague pictures of 'One Man And His Dog' flitted through my head. I really was too tired to care. (I didn't know it then but I was developing M.E. – chronic fatigue syndrome).

"Yes. And his name is Yo,"

Yo! I thought to myself. *That's a fine old Scottish name!* But I did not say this out loud. Instead, I blethered about sheep and the Scottish Highlands until the bus came in.

It was the local afternoon bus to Nazareth. We were going to stay with Ariela's cousin, Tmira, on a kibbutz at Hasholelim that night.

My Arab friend said goodbye politely – he called me Madam! – and went down the front of the bus to greet the driver while I went to the back with Ariela. I like the sunny side; she liked the shade so once again I sat alone, thinking about Yo.

What sort of a name was that? What could he have meant? *Yo.* Ewen, maybe? YO? Hugh! HUGH!

My cousin Hugh is a shepherd. He goes to Israel sometimes for a break from the boredom of wet sheep. It couldn't be Hugh, could it? He always goes to Eilat in the far south on the Gulf.

I told this to Ariela who got very excited. "You *must* ask him " she said. "Go and speak to him. Tell him."

So, once the giggling Arab boys had got off and there was more space, I walked down to the front of the bus and perched across the aisle behind the driver.

"Is this your friend?" I said, showing my Palestinian Hugh's name and address which I'd scribbled on a bit of paper.

He smiled. "I can't remember," he said, "Read it to me." It was only later I realised he probably could not read English though he spoke it very well.

"Do you think you know him?" he said.

"Perhaps."

"Let's play a game. Let's describe him."

"Right." I said. "You go first."

So, on the slow bus to Nazareth, stopping at every hill village along the crest, with everybody hanging on every word, including the driver, we played at describing Hugh.

People crept down the aisle to be nearer our conversation, Ariela among them.

"He's big." he said.

"Yes."

"He has broad shoulders."

"Yes."

"He plays a – " He mimed a penny whistle.

"Yes."

"He . . . " He closed his eyes, thinking, "He has fair hair and blue eyes and. . . . He opened them suddenly. "He looks like you!"

"So he should! He's my cousin!" I said.

The bus erupted with joy. "YAYYY!"

They were bouncing on the seats and cheering like the Muppet Show. Ariela was beside herself.

"And. . . ." he said triumphantly, "He has five sheepdogs!"

"They were parked in his pickup outside my house last week!"

It was the clincher. More yells of delight. I thought the bus would go off the road. The driver was steering it like a fairground ride, grinning back at us over his shoulder, enjoying the fun.

It was an amazing coincidence. Adel worked in Eilat and seldom came north. His home was near Nazareth and he had only been changing buses in Acco. I had been in Acco for one afternoon and would probably never be in Acco again.

He invited us to his home for tea but we were still a distance from Hasholelim and this was the last bus of the day. Regretfully we had to refuse.

Ariela spent hours on the phone that night telling her family the story.

"I'd give anything to see Hugh's face when you tell him about it and give him Adel's messages," she said.

"I can't wait myself."

But I had to.

When I got back to Skye I discovered that Hugh had headed off to Europe. I had to sit on the story for nearly a month.

Then one day, when the rain had been pouring in torrents for three long weeks, the phone rang. It was Nourit, Ariela's sister, whom I had last seen eating watermelon on her Tel Aviv rooftop as the sun went down in the Med. She was phoning from Bernera in the Outer Hebrides, standing in a shed in the rain waiting for the ferry! She wondered if we could meet.

Of course I went to the Uig ferry to meet her and took her home with me for a few days to try to repay some of the marvellous hospitality her family had given me.

Nourit does hair and wigs for the Israeli Opera and just after I had left Israel, the Opera left for Frankfurt. Backstage staff were not needed during rehearsal week so she took off for the remotest place she could find where she could be alone and walk anywhere without fear – the very opposite of Hugh and I.

We were sitting by the fire drinking tea when a pickup truck with five collie dogs in the back rolled up at the gate. Hugh was back at last.

So Ariela did not see his face when I told him my story.

But her sister did!

AFTER THE FUNERAL

The man with the aspidistra
stood in the pouring rain
while water sang in the gutters
and gurgled down the drain.
The taxis had all gone elsewhere.
No buses stopped in the street.
He was soaked to the skin
and his shoes let in
and the rain was turning to sleet.
His auntie had just been buried
and a will of sorts had been read.
Arrangements had all been completed
when a distant cousin said,
"Give George the aspidistra."
(They were handing round the tea.)
"Give George the aspidistra.
He could do with the company."
That cousin was gormless Norman,
a joker, a bit of a berk
And, thinking he'd put one over on George,
he looked around with a smirk.
The relatives giggled a little
and wriggled about in their chairs.
George tended to keep himself to himself
and some thought he gave himself airs.
But George had always liked auntie.
He was sorry that she was dead
so he turned to the aspidistra.
"Abide with me," he said
He knew they were taking the mickey

and decided enough was enough
so he picked up the pot and stalked out of the house
quite pleased he had called their bluff.
And found himself out in the suburbs,
a man in an empty street,
clutching an aspidistra
while the rain was turning to sleet.
But he grinned and pulled up his collar.
He cuddled his leathery load
and, peering through wet vegetation,
he trudged away home down the road.

CALUM'S ROAD

Squeak of the wheel and the clang of my hardy shovel,
Thud of the pick and the rattle of the stones;
Back-breaking labour, regardless of every weather,
Sweat in the summer and winter in my bones.

Fortune revolves like the wheel of my barrow rolling
Over the rocks and the hard unyielding ground.
Good times and bad; there are days when I feel defeated,
Just plodding on till a better day comes round.

Uphill and downhill and all round another corner,
Starting at Brochel, four thousand yards to go
Through Rainy's wall and on to my home in Arnish.
Lobbied for a road but the Councillors said, No.

Fortune revolves like the wheel of my barrow rolling
Over the rocks and the hard unyielding ground.
Good times and bad; there are days when I feel defeated,
Just plodding on till a better day comes round.

Rocks can be tough and this landscape is old and stubborn.
I'm of this land and I'm strong and stubborn too.
A wee bit today, then a bit more I'll make tomorrow;
Footstep by footstep I'm going to win through.

Lyrics composed to Donald Shaw's tune, Calum's Road

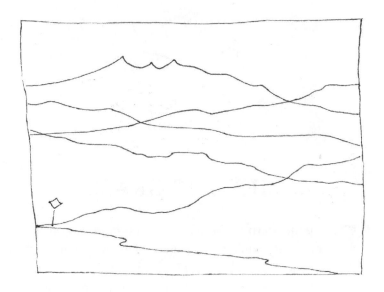

Calum Macleod (1911-1988) lived on the island of Raasay between Skye and Wester Ross. His native township of Arnish had petitioned for a cart-track in1925 to link them to the public road but had been refused and the population declined. Calum remained as keeper of the Rona Lighthouse nearby. He continued to feel passionately that he had a right to a road to his home and in 1966, since no help was forthcoming, he set about building a road himself. Single-track. Single-handed. He wore out ten years, two wheelbarrows, six picks, six shovels, four spades and five hammers in the making and in 1976 had the satisfaction of seeing his famous road tarred by the Council.

LIKE THE GRASS

The potted fern in the window shot its fronds out like a firework, a dynamic force, eagerly defying gravity, zipping up and out. Behind it the old lady sat rooted in her chair, bedded into the fabric by pain. She was watching and waiting for a glimpse of people passing – anybody. And when there was nobody she watched time pass. Soon the schoolchildren would be coming out, bags bumping, lunch-boxes swinging. They would be a gleam of music, a chord of light in her prison.

The clock struggled with the quarter. It longed to sing out the time but its Westminster chimes had been restrained so it whirred and fluttered, went clunk, then patiently resumed its ticking.

Her knitting slid down the side of her chair and her hands rested, weary on her lap. The sock was nearly finished – socks for her grandson, enormous socks now. How could anyone who had been so small the other day have size eleven feet? But her daughter had said so on the phone. Maybe tomorrow someone would call in and post them for her. He'd be needing them.

She looked down at her hands, gently massaging the pain in her joints. They were gnarled and knobby, the skin seamed and swollen, finger-tips askew with arthritis. "You know things as well as the back of your hand," she thought, " but how well is that? So many hands have lain in my lap over the years – a stranger's hands now, yet once I must have known them as well as myself."

Her thoughts became confused. Pictures came and went; soft vulnerable childish hands with grubby questing fingers and bitten nails; girlish hands, smooth and manicured, smelling of lotion, hands to be held, hands for stroking. The left hand had acquired a ring, a thin gold band that had slipped easily on and had had to be cut off when her knuckles grew so distorted. Housewife's hands, mother's hands, forever busy, smoothing, scouring, sorting out messes, gradually assuming the signs of hard labour, palm lines etching deeper with the passing years. Hands that were taken for granted until the first twinges of arthritis punished her complacency. Now these hands were unruly members, stiff, stuck, impossible to ignore.

"These are old hands," she thought. "They are all worn out. I don't want them any more."

Many women sat in the chair beside the fern. Many women peered through the tunnel of her vision at the empty street. The tunnel shafted inwards.

She saw a bride dancing with orange blossom in her hair, her veil looped over her arm. She wore a creamy-white dress with a froth of lace round her shoulders, smooth pearls at her throat. She raised her hands to her neck but the pearls were gone; the skin was slack.

Was the bride herself or her daughter? Two brides danced laughing among the shadowy guests.

She saw a young teacher facing a class, reading with a child, mending a cut knee. The children belonged to no particular year but were an amalgamation of all the best-remembered characters in her long term of teaching. Strange how some children maintained a niche in your memory while others simply vanished. Not just the clever ones, not just the stupid ones – the personalities remained. Names and faces came and went and she greeted them – elderly people now whom she would not recognise.

She had good times then, young lassie that she was.

Daft times. Happy times.

There was the time she got a lift in a posh car from some do or other. It was chauffeur-driven and she was squashed into the back. The journey was long and her friends were asleep but she was too shy to admit how sick she was feeling as the grand limousine sped up and down the sway-backed road. At last in desperation she had taken off her new cloche hat and was sick into it. Then she wound down the window and pitched the whole thing out into the dark.

"Nobody noticed," the old lady told the fern. " My good hat!"

Time slipped down the faults and crevices of memory. There was the house where they were first married, glowing in the sun, a homely house with hens clucking, apple trees, Davy's neat rows of vegetables.

She remembered her proud rows of tulips planted by the path and her toddling daughter breaking off the "pretty cups" to bring to Mammy.

Her head drooped and she thought about Davy, her husband – an old man – a strong young man in tweed plus-fours, a slender good-looking man with black hair. She remembered the comfort of him in the night but she could not isolate the men one from another because change is so gradual, so imperceptible. We flow from one person to another as quiet as the tide.

Suddenly she caught the memory of his pipe and the whiff of St Bruno Flake evoked him vividly in his mid-thirties, still playing shinty, vital and exciting. Shinty and his boat and his garden – these were his recreations and he gave them up in that order as age advanced. He was planting tatties when the stroke took him.

Pictures on the screen of her closed eyelids.

Dark figures round the grave on a sunny day, wind whipping the daffodils and coat-tails and hair. Too good a day to be planted underground but a grand day for the garden. The sky should have been mourning on sleek umbrellas.

One by one she had seen her friends go before her. Once her man was away she had to see herself as a single entity, to make decisions for nobody but herself. It was hardly worth the bother. Still, losing Davy had not been all that sad. Queer that! It was a relief of a kind. A consummation. The fullness of time. Man going to his long home.

"Something attempted, something done
To earn a night's repose . . ."

That was what Davy used to say. And that was what he had done. He had earned his night's repose. He'd had a good life, a very good life.

"And so have I," she said aloud, suddenly raising her head to the window. The fern quivered, sympathetic to the vibrations.

"A good man and a good life."

The school bell wrecked the peace. There was a pause, then footsteps pattered along the street. One or two faces turned to the window with the fern. Two little boys made a rude sign and ran away giggling. A little girl waved shyly.

The old lady smiled and her hands fluttered crookedly. She laid back her head and closed her eyes. The fire spurted and settled again. Time passed softly in the drowsy room and quietly, very quietly, the tick of the clock faded away.

MEMORY

a canvas
made of living tissue
on which we paint
our scenery of dreams.

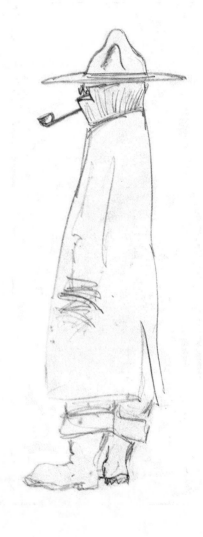

Rev. Mackinnon watching a shinty match

Dream for Alpin

What did you see
When the cresses closed over your head
And you sank out of sight
In Tobar na h-Anait?
Did your blind eyes
Fill with mud?
Or did you see the magic fish
Dart golden
Through the crystal water,
Rainbow-shadowed
Under its green canopy
As you descended
To the underworld,
The otherworld of dreams
Where legends live
And time pays homage
To eternity?

Morag Henriksen, a Ross from Ross-shire, grew up in Lochcarron and at Dingwall Academy and was a teacher in Edinburgh, Portree and Uig.

An artist, poet and singer, she has lived on the Isle of Skye since 1967 and has two sons, Ross and Scott, both artists.

GLOSSARY

Aoibhneas   Delight

Landscape with Figures
Morbheann   Big hill

The Burning Fiery Furnace
Bokes   retches
Dunt   a thump, a nudge with the elbow

Outside Lavvies
Scunnered   disgusted, fed up

Scapegoat
Craitur   creutair bochd, Gaelic for poor thing

Saved
The Mod   Annual Scottish Gaelic music competition.

Mrs Cameron
Cùram   the change, a conversion
Dwalm   a trance
Turas   a journey, a circuit, a pilgrimage
A ghràidh   dear, dearest

Landscape with Sheep
Bodach   old man
Gonadh ort!   (Gaelic expletive) Blast it!
Isd thu!   Be quiet!
Greas ort!   Get a move on! Hurry up.

Chaneil thu glic	You are not wise. You're daft.
A bhronag	poor wee thing, an endearment
Morach	saltings, turf covered by sea at high tide
Slake	mud uncovered at low tide
Clegs	horse-flies

Bonnie George Campbell

Laigh	low
Blethering	chattering volubly
Leòdhasach	a man from Lewis
Machair	grassland between sandy beach and peat bog
Mo rùn geal òg	My fair young love

Over the Sea to Where?

Slàinte!	Health!
Avernus	a volcanic crater lake near Cumae in Italy, believed to be the entrance to the Underworld
Erebus	a region of the Underworld where the dead went immediately after dying
Asphodel Fields	a neutral place where ghosts who had been neither very good or very bad were held
Styx	the river of death separating Earth and the Underworld
Charon	the ferryman over the Styx
Acheron	a tributary of the Styx sometimes ferried by Charon
Phlegethon	the torrid river of fire, another Stygian tributary
Lethe	the river of forgetfulness
Loch Hourn	Loch Iuthairne, Loch of Hell
Loch Nevis	Loch Nimheis, Loch of Heaven
Burd	girl

The Tairsgeir

Tairsgeir   turf knife, peat-iron

The Soft Present

Zimmer   a walking-frame

The Bad Step

Bothy   a hut, a shelter

Mrs Miller

Laochan   (Gaelic endearment) Little hero

The Brahan Seer

Coinneach Odhar   Pale Kenneth

The Slug Bonus

Dosser   someone who sleeps rough
Lobey Dosser   a cartoon strip by Bud Neill
Teuchter   a Highlander (derogatory Lowland term)
Scunner   disgust, a nuisance

Johnny Com

Crack   good conversation

Pink Paint

Annus horribilis   a horrible year
Dies horribilissima   the most horrible day

More About the Fetish

Seannachie   a storyteller, (G *seanchaidh*)
Mîle Marbhaisg   a thousand curses (on love)
Waulking   beating wet tweed rhythmically to shrink it
Bodhran   drum used in Celtic music
Buisneach   the evil eye

Peatsmoke

Falaisgean	muirburn, heather-burning
Ceilidh	a visit often with story, song or dancing
The Broch	An Iron Age drystone hollow-walled tower, peculiar to Scotland
Fank	a sheepfold